The Adventures of New Grandma

The Adventures of New Grandma

Jim Pahz

The Adventures of New Grandma
© Jim Pahz 2015

Published by

ISBN - 978-0-9886423-6-2

FOREWORD

This is the story of Marilyn Miller, lovingly referred to as New Grandma. She is a soft spoken, unobtrusive woman, an avid reader, who likes to do needlepoint. By nature she is humble, and would prefer to live her life in the background so as not be noticed.

For Marilyn, the state of the world doesn't matter, except in the most abstract sense. Current events, politics, national interests, technological changes—all of these things are relatively unimportant. What matters to Marilyn is family. That's the way it always has been, and that's the way it remains.

Marilyn was married for fifty-five years. She spent twenty years in retirement in Panama City, Florida. After her husband, Morris, passed away, she was alone in Florida. She was sad and lonely. So Hannah and I persuaded her to come to Michigan where she could be integrated into our family and be loved and cherished during her remaining years.

Marilyn is the mother of my wife, Hannah. This story describes the road our family traveled once New Grandma joined us in Michigan.

My name is Daniel Savidge. Hannah and I have two daughters (grown) and three grandsons. We live on 40 acres in Central Michigan—the *Middle of the Mitten*. We also have twenty peacocks roaming freely, a few chickens, three cats, and a dog. Hannah and I are both employed. I am a professor of Public Health Education at a local university, and Hannah works in the university library.

CHAPTER ONE

The Third Act

Some people refer to the time of life after parenting and careers are finished as *the third act*. Others call it the *encore years*. It is the thirty or so years added to a person's lifespan as a result of modern technology and better health care practices. I think of the folk singer *Phil Ochs* and believe he was referring to this period when he sang about taking the *pleasures of the harbor*.

I mention him because Marilyn Miller, was a fan of his. When she reached her encore years, she wasn't having much pleasure. The harbor wasn't inviting enough. She was a widow, and she was lonely.

Marilyn didn't really want to come to Michigan, and she was conflicted. Alone in the Florida panhandle, there was insufficient sunshine to ease the pain of her loss. So at our request, she migrated north to be close to her only daughter. She told me once, "I didn't want to move here. I only did it because I want to be close to family. Michigan is too cold and there's too much snow. The climate in Florida is better. I love Panama City."

Our grandchildren were curious about this new addition to the family and what to call her. Since they already had a grandma, we explained it by saying, "This is your new grandma. She is Grandma's mother." This was as good an explanation as an eight and a five-year-old needed. Henceforth, Marilyn Miller, my wife's mother, and my mother-in-law, became known to our family as *New Grandma*.

At that time, Marilyn weighed 102 pounds, which caused my wife and me to be concerned. Hannah and I asked her to move in with us, but she refused. "I don't want to be a burden, I can live alone and take care of myself," she exclaimed defiantly. We asked her again and again, but her answer was always the same.

So Marilyn moved into a rent-subsidized housing complex called *Canterbury Gardens*. She was happy there. The housing unit was only one block from *Target* and when the weather was warm she could walk to the store to shop. She was comfortable with her elderly neighbors who lived at the Gardens, and immediately began making friends.

Unfortunately, the harmony of her new living accommodations didn't last long because the State of Michigan decided to close the state home for the developmentally disabled. Housing was needed for the population who resided there, and many of the people were relocated to the *Canterbury Gardens*. These people seemed odd—different from the residents who lived at the Gardens. But the state needed to put these people somewhere, and the *Canterbury Gardens* was selected. The residents were not happy. They couldn't understand why these people needed to be housed at the *Canterbury Gardens*. There was much speculation and the consensus of opinion was that closing down the state facility was a cost saving measure. Whatever the reason, the move infuriated many residents, including Marilyn.

Nevertheless, Marilyn's third act began on a high note. She was an *active senior*, although she still chain-smoked. Neither Hannah nor I smoked cigarettes and that resulted in some minor inconveniences for New Grandma. For example, we asked if she could refrain from smoking when in the car with us, or from smoking inside our house. She didn't like it, but she complied.

New Grandma, Hannah, and I got along well together. In the summers we would travel around the state looking for adventure. The trips were short, usually one to three days, where the three of us visited places of interest.

Those first summers together we visited Caseville for the annual Cheeseburger Festival, and encouraged New Grandma to eat cheeseburgers. We weren't very subtle in our attempts to get her to eat, and that week New Grandma might have actually put on a little weight. In Shepherd we attended the

Maple Syrup Festival, and pleaded with New Grandma to eat pancakes. Afterward we walked around the community looking for antiques. We traveled to Traverse City for the national Cherry Festival, Saugatuck to look at art, and Holly Grove to watch knights joust at the Renaissance Festival in September. There are many festivals in Michigan. The summer is festival time. The trips were highly enjoyable to Hannah and me, as well as New Grandma, and I believe they helped lift her spirits and lessen the pain of leaving Florida.

In New Grandma's third year with us we visited the Tulip Festival in Holland, Michigan. We were walking around admiring the beautiful plantings.

"Mom," Hannah said. "You're coughing a lot. You need to stop smoking, or at least cut down on those cigarettes."

"I know," New Grandma said. "You know how many times your father and I quit, probably a thousand. I'm addicted. I think that's the nature of addiction—even if you want to quit you can't.

You simply lose control over your ability to stop."

"Well, when we get back to Mount Pleasant, Mom, I want you to make an appointment with a doctor. Go see Dr. Goldfeder about that cough. And while we're there we should also ask him about your weight. You're too thin, Mom. Daniel and I worry."

"Ok, I promise. But when we get back to Mount Pleasant, I want to stop at *Staples*. I need a few office supplies."

"Of course," I said. "We can do that. What do you need?"

"Writing pads… a few pens. It's not that I *need* anything, really, but I like looking. I always appreciate office supplies. It's too bad I don't have an office. That would give me an excuse to keep buying supplies."

"You don't need an excuse. We can stop, and you can pretend you have an office."

"Can we also stop at JoAnn fabrics? I need some needlepoint stuff."

"Of course," I answered.

"Look at all these beautiful tulips, There must be thousands of them. They're incredible."

"It's really something to see," Hannah added. "I like the way they separate the flower beds according to color and type."

"Do you know how you hear on the news at night about the housing market crashing, how the newscasters refer to it as the collapse of the housing bubble?"

"Yes," I answered.

"Well, it is a bubble," New Grandma said. "Houses were overpriced and the credit-worthiness of buyers insufficient. Mortgage banks lowered their requirements for buyers. But it wasn't the first bubble. Historically speaking there were previous bubbles. The collapse of the tulip bubble is one example."

"What do you mean?" I asked.

New Grandma continued. "You see," she said, "there was a time in the Dutch history when the people went literally crazy for tulips. I think it happened in the 1600s. The price of tulip bulbs shot up so high that a single bulb would equal the cost of a house—and I mean a nice house, one you would be proud to live in. Speculators began to buy and sell tulips in hopes of making easy money. People became obsessed with tulips and fortunes were made. Historians refer to the phenomenon as tulipmania. But you see," New Grandma continued, "a bubble is nothing more than an artificially inflated market—and bubbles burst. It was inevitable that this would happen, and it did in Holland. Many people lost all their money.

"In subsequent years the tulip remained popular as a beautiful flower, but not as an investment. The price dropped to prices similar to that of other pretty flowers. But to the Dutch people the tulip remained special and still does. Do you know that more than a billion bulbs are shipped annually from Holland? Whenever Dutch people immigrate to other parts of the world, they usually bring tulips with them. So it was the descendants of Dutch settlers that decided to purchase and plant 100,000 tulip bulbs in Holland, Michigan, early in twentieth century. They started this tulip festival that continues to this day."

"I had no idea," I said. "How do you know about it?"

"I've always loved to read," New Grandma said, "and I love history. My ancestry is German/ Dutch so I was aware of the tulip situation since childhood. Actually, the Dutch were not the first to go bonkers for tulips." She paused to light another cigarette. "It happened even earlier in Turkey, in the 1500s. Turkey, as you know, was part of the Ottoman Empire and was the first country to start tulip festivals. Historians call it *The Age of Tulips,* and it is said at that time, a tulip was more valuable than a person's life. The tulip was the symbol of success and prestige. Everyone wanted to own tulips. So when you hear on the news that the housing bubble burst, or the technology bubble, or any other kind of bubble, it's nothing new. It happened before and it will happen again. History has a way of repeating itself." New Grandma started to cough.

"Just think," I said, "now you can go into a

discount store and buy a sack of tulip bulbs for about ten dollars. Things certainly change."

"Yes they do," New Grandma said between coughs. "Change is the only constant. For example, who would have thought I would ever be back in Michigan? I started out here, and now I've ended up here."

"And if you don't quit smoking, you'll be buried here," I said. "Besides, Michigan isn't so bad. I read on a postcard once that three out of five Great Lakes prefer Michigan—not Florida—Michigan. That should tell you something."

"It does. And I've got to admit I've never seen tulips as glorious as these Michigan tulips in Florida. Under the right conditions Michigan is almost perfect, but that's only in the summers and fall. The winters suck, and the spring can go either way. But each summer I look forward to these little trips we take together—our mini vacations. Where are we going next summer?"

"Well, there's a castle in Charlevoix. We haven't gone yet to Mackinac Island, and we really should. That's a fascinating place to visit. No cars on the island, only horse-drawn vehicles. There's the vineyards on the west side of the state, Greenfield Village to the south. We haven't scratched the surface. There are still lots of places to visit."

"I'm so glad," New Grandma said. "I wish Morris could be here with us to enjoy our excursions. I think he would have loved them."

Hannah reached out and took her mother's hand. "He would have, but it's just the three of us now so we'll have to enjoy them for Dad also. I'm sure if there's a heaven Dad is watching and enjoying our little adventures. He's probably bored up there. Can you picture him sitting around day after day trying to master the rudiments of the harp. Learning about tulips has got to be more interesting than harp technique. Now promise me you'll call Dr. Goldfeder and make an appointment—after we visit the office supply store."

"Pie."

"What?"

"Pie." New Grandma repeated.

"What about pie?"

"We should make a pie… an apple pie. And we should make it from scratch. I don't want any store-bought pie. And I don't want to get one from the bakery. I want to make it ourselves."

"Ok. We'll make a pie. When do you want to eat it?"

"Memorial Day. I have a hunger for pie, and Memorial Day will be here soon."

"Ok Mom. Let me check our agenda. When we get home we will first go to *Staples* and *JoAnn* fabrics. Next we will make an appointment with Dr. Goldfeder. When we get together for the Memorial Day holiday, we will make a pie—from scratch. Is that everything? Do I have it correctly?"

"Perfect, Hannah. You got it right."

CHAPTER TWO

Hannah's Adoption

A week later New Grandma had her appointment with the doctor.

"Mrs. Miller," the doctor said, "you are too thin—way too thin. Your surgical procedure is scheduled for next week. I would feel better if you had a little more meat on your bones."

"I know. My weight is a problem."

"Yes, it is. I want you to gain weight. You need to eat more."

"That's what they say." She pointed to Hannah and me. "They think they are the food police. They're always telling me to eat more. I eat all the time. I also take two bottles of *Ensure* every day. They are always bringing me *Ensure*."

"That's good. Make it three bottles," the doctor said. "But that's in addition to food. You need more calories. I'm going to prescribe an appetite stimulant for you. The cough concerns me," Dr. Goldfeder continued. "You shouldn't smoke. You know that—everybody knows that. It is a terrible habit."

"I know, doctor, but I've smoked my whole life. It's hard to give it up."

"I understand, but you must try. I can prescribe a nicotine patch if you're willing to make the effort. But for it to work, you have to be serious. You have to really want to stop smoking."

"I don't think I'm ready for a patch. I promise I'll try and cut down."

"Well," the doctor said, "that's a start."

Looking at Marilyn, I could tell she wasn't a happy camper. We left the doctor's office and stopped at a restaurant for some lunch. We were sitting in a corner booth in the darkest part of the restaurant.

"I can't believe he wants me to drink more of that stuff," New Grandma said. "I don't even like the way it tastes. Maybe I should go to a different doctor."

In an effort to change the subject, Hannah asked,

"Mom, was I adopted?"

"What? What are you talking about?" Marilyn replied.

"Daniel says I might be adopted."

She looked at me and scowled. "What would he know? He wasn't there."

"Yes, but he's pointed out an interesting fact. He says he's never seen a baby picture of me. That could be because I was adopted and therefore there were no baby pictures."

"Nonsense. What a dumb thing to say."

"There's nothing wrong with being adopted," Hannah continued. "I wouldn't mind if I was, and I wouldn't love you any less. My children are adopted and I don't love them less."

"I know that, but no, you're not adopted. And how can you ask such a silly question a week before I'm scheduled for surgery?"

Marilyn's surgery was to correct a vascular condition in her leg, and Dr. Goldfeder said it was a routine procedure, and there was no need to worry.

"The last time you rode in our Prius," Hannah

said, "you didn't weigh enough to cause the airbag sign to illuminate on the dashboard. Even the car thinks you don't weigh enough, Mother. I think the car is trying to tell you something. Maybe that's the second opinion you're looking for." The comment annoyed Marilyn, but I laughed. She shot me one of those looks like she was about to vomit. Marilyn seemed to be in an especially bad mood today—the doctor's advice and the wrong restaurant.

"I hate this place," Marilyn said. She looked around the restaurant. "The food is awful, and the place has no ambiance. It reminds me of the *Korean Palace*. One bite and I had enough. Everything tasted the same. No matter what you ordered, it all tasted the same—remember? Actually, I don't like foreign food. Who knows what kind of creepy-crawly things you're getting when you eat that stuff."

"That's silly," I said. "There's nothing wrong with eating foreign food, and there's nothing creepy or disgusting in it. It's just different—that's all. Eating foreign food is an adventure. It's fun."

"Not for me. I'm not eating at the Korean Palace,

or the Mumbai Grill. If I ever go to Vanuatu I'm not eating their vittles either. I don't want an adventure when I go out to eat. I want predictability. I want dishes that taste good. Do you know, Daniel, that in China people eat dogs?"

"Really?"

"Yes, really. In Yulin there's a dog meat festival. I saw a report about it on CNN: they eat *dog with tofu,* and *crispy dog.* One of the more popular dishes is called *dog hot pot.* It's supposed to taste best when it's spicy. Doesn't that sound yummy? Tell me Daniel, would you want to eat Fido?"

"What about pizza?"

"What about it?"

"It's Italian. That's foreign."

"Pizza doesn't count. There are exceptions to every rule, and my rule is that if you take me to a foreign restaurant I'm not going to eat."

"You don't eat, no matter where we take you."

"I don't eat if I'm not hungry. And no, you're not adopted—of course you're not. That's the most ridiculous thing I've heard all day."

"Maybe, but you must admit it looks suspicious.

I don't have baby pictures."

"I told you, the pictures were stolen. They were in a box in the garage. It was forty years ago when we lived in Chattanooga, and the box was stolen."

"You never told me that."

"I did. I told you several times."

"I don't remember you ever telling me."

"It's true. We were living in Chattanooga and your father was working for the 3-M company. If he was alive, he would confirm it. I have your birth certificate as proof."

"I've never seen one single baby picture of me before the age of two. I don't think either set of grandparents had any pictures, nor my aunts, uncles, or cousins. Don't you think that's strange? You've got to admit it's unusual. Daniel thinks it's bizarre."

"You want to know what's bizarre? You don't have to look any further than your husband. He's bizarre."

"Adopted children have birth certificates," Hannah continued. "Callie has one."

"Are you saying I'm a bad mother?"

"No, of course not. I'm saying there are no pictures of me as a baby. That's all."

"I told you they were stolen from a box in the garage."

Hannah paused, then asked, "Why would someone steal a box of pictures from our garage? Who would want them? What good could they possibly do a stranger, who wouldn't know any of the people in the pictures? Do you think there is a black market in baby pictures?"

"You're being a smart-ass," Marilyn said, "I told you they were stolen."

"And why were they in the garage in the first place? Why weren't they in a picture album on a coffee table or in a bookcase? Why weren't they inside the house?"

"Because we had just moved. All our stuff was in boxes in the garage and we hadn't gotten to that box to put the things away. I think there was a box of needlepoint supplies. It was a long time ago. But I remember I was working on a mountain scene. All my supplies were stolen—along with the other stuff."

"The pictures?"

"The pictures were packed with other things. I don't think the thief was after pictures of you as a baby; he was probably after anything he could get. He didn't know what was in the box. It was sealed." Marilyn paused and turned towards me. "This is your theory?" She turned to Hannah. "He is always stirring things up—this husband of yours. That's what he does; he is an instigator. He likes to agitate and get things going."

"Well," Hannah said, "You've got to admit it's a plausible theory. No baby pictures, not a single one. I think Daniel had reason to be suspicious. And this doesn't have anything to do with your surgery. Just because you are going to the hospital doesn't mean we can't talk about other things."

"No, it means you shouldn't upset me. I'm an old lady, and sensitive."

CHAPTER THREE

A Philosophy of Mothers-in-Law

My friend Norman told me he had one rule regarding his mother-in-law—she wasn't allowed in his house...period, end of story, nothing more to discuss! Norman was a Rotarian, and I ate dinner with him at our weekly meeting of Rotary International.

Norman owned a hardware store in town, appropriately named *Norman's Hardware*. He was well thought of within the community, and had worked hard on Rotary's *Polio Plus* campaign, as well as local projects.

One night over dinner I said, "The motto of Rotary is *service above self*. How can you reconcile that guiding principle with the way you treat your mother-in-law?"

"I can't," Norman replied. "I guess I'm a hypocrite. Anyway, there are always exceptions to any rule. My mother-in-law is highly detestable. I can't stand to be around her."

"I see," I answered. I might add here as a postscript, that Norman is now divorced. His policy regarding mothers-in-law didn't work out so well. It wasn't conducive to a happy marriage. The divorce left him bitter and estranged from his son. I admonished Norman, "See," I said. "If a man is so insensitive and cruel to another human being, his wife will leave him. It was inevitable. What goes around comes around."

"That's a cliché."

"Yes, it is, but you should have followed the Rotary motto and treated her better." I thought I was being wise and morally superior. But the reality was I didn't know his mother-in-law. So it was easy for me to be self-righteous, and pontificate about how Norman should have behaved. I was, in other words, full of crap.

Flash forward ten years to when my own mother-in-law came to Michigan. Before moving to Michigan, Marilyn always seemed a lovely woman. She was attractive, demure, and soft spoken. That perception didn't change after her arrival, but as she became more and more integrated into our lives I realized she was a person not unlike everyone else. She wasn't perfect, but had her strengths and weaknesses as we all do.

Although Marilyn started her third act strong, she soon began to show the effects of aging. She stopped driving her car. Her vision declined and bright light hurt her eyes. Every time we went to a restaurant she requested they lower the blinds. Her other faculties also began to diminish. I think she probably had an eating disorder. No, there's no thinking involved: she had an eating disorder. She also had a swollen foot which she liked to talk about, and Dr. Goldfeder diagnosed her recently with chronic obstructive pulmonary disease (COPD). It's a diagnosis she refused to accept. The doctor insisted she stop smoking and eventually, he put her on oxygen.

***

In her housing unit, Marilyn is always cold. She sets the thermostat to the maximum level. The temperature rises in excess of 80 degrees, but it is still too cold for her, so she supplements the heat by dressing in two layers of clothing and using a space heater. I guess that's what happens when there is no meat on your bones— no insulation. Of course, the apartment is too warm for most people so Marilyn doesn't get a lot of visitors; when she does, the visits are brief and when the guests leave, they look like potted plants deprived of water. Even the Jehovah's Witnesses have stopped coming around. I'm sure the reason is it's hard to discuss the gospel when you're melting.

Marilyn sits in her over-heated apartment and worries. She has become a frequent complainer. Day by day Marilyn's list of grievances grows. Sometimes her complaints seem valid, like the one against her neighbor, Morton Nicholes. Mr. Nicholes lives down the hall with three cats, in violation of the policy against pet ownership. Occasionally he lets his cats loose in the hallway so they can exercise. But in order to keep them from running away he closes the steel fire-door at the end of the hall. The door is heavy and is not supposed to be closed unless there is a fire; then the door closes automatically. Most of the residents are old and don't have the strength to open the door. It angers Marilyn who says if there is a fire they will all burn up.

"Then why don't you talk to your neighbor?" I ask.

"He won't listen. His cats mean everything to him."

"Then complain to the management."

"I can't do that. I'm a good neighbor. Besides, I think he's schizophrenic—you know—crazy." Marilyn makes a fist and taps it against her forehead. "He's one of those fruit-loops they moved in from the state home. Those people don't generally obey the rules. Besides, does it really matter if we all burn up? The *Canterbury Gardens* is God's waiting room. We're all just waiting for the grim reaper to come and get us while our feet swell."

JIM PAHZ

CHAPTER FOUR

Antipathy

Sometimes I think my mother-in-law hates me. I suspect this because she is always criticizing me. Then she follows her criticism by saying, "You know I love you." She criticizes me for eating too much. She says I eat too fast. I am incapable of relaxing, and am always in a race with time. I make her nervous. And, although I am in a hurry, I am, according to her, quite lazy by nature, and have never worked more than four hours a day in my life. "That is evident," she says "because you take naps in the afternoon." And sometimes, I do.

I explain to Marilyn that I live on a farm, which, of course, she knows. Hannah and I have been surrounded by animals our whole lives. We've had dogs, cats, horses, all sorts of pets. I've watched them and I've observed that when animals are tired they stop whatever it is they're doing and go to sleep. "People are no different than animals," I say. "There is nothing wrong in taking a nap. It's good for you. Sleep is important. That's my philosophy when the body is tired, stop and rest."

"That's an excuse," Marilyn says, "not a philosophy. You're not an animal, although sometimes you share certain traits with animals. I had a cat like you once. Its name was *Perspicacious*, but I usually just called him *Percy*, He was the laziest cat you ever saw-sleeping all the time. All he ever wanted to do was sleep."

"Was he an old cat?"

"No, just lazy. A lot like you, Daniel."

Marilyn says I have always been overpaid for what little work I have done. I am a professor and don't wear a business suit or carry a tool box. She says I am selfish and have the kind of personality that drives people crazy. She doesn't understand how Hannah can put up with me (I've wondered that myself, at times). One thing I have learned from listening to Marilyn is, if your mother-in-law criticizes you and then follows it up by saying how much she loves you, beware. Be skeptical; she may hold you in contempt. She also complains that Hannah and I keep the temperature in our house too cold.

"That's why I don't want to visit," Marilyn says.

I protest, "We keep our house at 70 degrees, and when you visit I turn the thermostat to 75. That should be more than sufficient."

"It's not. It's always cold there!"

"I can't keep it as warm as your apartment. You set it higher than 80 degrees. That's okay if you're a tropical plant, like an orchid, but not if you're a human being."

"You don't understand, I have to wear two layers of clothes and I'm still cold."

"I'm sorry, but it's because you are too thin. Remember what the doctor said? You need to gain weight. You should eat more."

"Doctors don't know everything. Look at you. You're a doctor and you don't know anything."

"I'm not that kind of a doctor. I'm not a

physician. Anyone can see you are underweight."

"Oh please. Don't start with the eating thing again. It's tedious, and besides, I eat all the time."

"Of course you do."

***

Sometimes I have a hard time not losing my patience with Marilyn. I want to scream and shake her. I want to tell her she looks like a public service announcement for an eating disorder. Of course I don't say these things, even if they're true. I remain silent and keep my frustrations hidden.

Hannah reminds me, again, that Marilyn really loves me. "She doesn't mean anything by her comments. She has a hard time articulating her feelings, and just blurts out whatever she feels in the moment. She is really very sweet," Hannah says, "but she is old. You need to have patience."

I understand. I realize it sucks to be old. Everybody knows that. Marilyn reminds me of an old Buick I once owned. The car literally fell apart—piece by piece. First to go was the cooling system, then, the suspension; the engine always leaked oil and smoked terribly. Finally the transmission fell out. That's New Grandma in a nutshell—an old Buick that has seen better days, but keeps on sputtering.

***

Another thing of which I am critical regarding Marilyn is her indecisiveness. I don't know if she was always like this or if she developed the tendency in later life, but she is really indecisive today. The smallest decision seems to be exceedingly difficult. Ordering a meal at a restaurant becomes a major negotiation. Can broccoli be substituted for peas? Would they let her have rye bread instead of white bread? Does the house salad dressing taste like Italian dressing? If not, then what does it taste like? Would it be possible to have a sample? It usually takes Marilyn five minutes before she reaches a settlement with the waitress or waiter. This occurs even though she eats in the same restaurant, repeatedly, and knows the menu by heart. She cannot order a meal without going through this routine. It's like she is reciting a script or auditioning for a play. Then, when food comes she pushes it around her plate, cuts it into fractional parts, and asks for a box so she can take it home for the dog. Of course, she doesn't have a dog. I have never once seen Marilyn eat an entire meal. I think if I did I would send the news to *Ripley's Believe It or Not*. I'm quite sure they would reply: *impossible*.

Marilyn exhibits similar indecisiveness when shopping. She spends an hour or two trying to decide which pants to buy, and the following day calls Hannah to return them. Clothes never fit right—either too tight or too loose. Surprisingly, although Marilyn never wants to draw attention to herself, she is incredibly fashion-conscious. But she wants to wear the fashion of her youth, and it can be difficult finding toreador pants.

And then there's the increasing negativity. Since moving from Florida, Marilyn has reached the conclusion that the world is not such a good place. Everything in the past was better than today, and the future is too bleak to contemplate.

She likes to reminisce about Florida and the state's citrus products. She says Florida produces the best oranges and tomatoes. Some of her observations are undoubtedly true, but a lot of what she says seems exaggerated, a distortion of her life when her husband was alive. I think it is *selective recall*. She remembers the good things about her past while screening out unpleasant memories. That's probably a normal thing to do as people age. I assume we all do it.

One of the things Marilyn does enjoy is subscribing to magazines about the ideal life of yester-year. Magazines like *Reminisce* and *The Good Old Days* are filled with pictures of family life before computers, iPods, smart phones, and drones. Barbara Billingsley, who played June Cleaver in *Leave it to Beaver*, and Jane Wyatt as Margaret Anderson from *Father Knows Best,* are frequently remembered.

As Marilyn reads the articles about the past, she becomes more contemptuous of modern life. Like a glass of milk left outside of the refrigerator, she turns sour. With her frequent complaints, she begins to resemble a stereotype of an old person one might see portrayed in a Hollywood film—obstinate, cranky, and full of condemnation—an old codger. Her mantra is, "Wait until you're my age. Everything will be abundantly clear when you're 77. Then you'll understand." Maybe I will.

Lately, I haven't seen much of my wife. She is always running errands for her mother. Hannah is called repeatedly to fix her mother's computer, which is never really broken. Because Hannah and I are always trying to get Marilyn to eat, we have designated *adventure in restaurant days*. We also bring her cases of *Ensure* or anything else with which we can tempt her. Marilyn has become dependent on Hannah for most of the necessities of life. That she needs her daughter is understandable, but I must confess sometimes I get resentful of the time Hannah spends taking care of her. I can be selfish.

These days Norman asks me, "So what do you think now since Marilyn landed her broomstick at your door? How sympathetic to mothers-in-law are you now? From what I can deduce, Marilyn is a first rate pain-in-the-ass."

I stand there not knowing how to respond. Is Norman right? Does he see something I fail to recognize? Finally, I say, "She didn't come on a broom, she flew Delta."

*Made from scratch the Memorial Day
apple pie was a huge success for Hannah
and New Grandma.*

CHAPTER FIVE

Teeth in a Jar

I didn't realize how sensitive New Grandma was until an incident occurred over a poem I had written. It was silly, really. One day our grandsons, Erik and Josh, confided to me that while visiting New Grandma's apartment they had seen some teeth in a jar in the bathroom. I told them they were New Grandma's teeth—her dentures.

"What are dentures?" Erik asked.

"False teeth."

"Why does New Grandma have false teeth?"

"Because of the secrets."

"Secrets?"

"Yes, New Grandma has so many secrets they sometimes make her mouth sore. She can't hold them all. One day her teeth complained and asked if they could come out of her mouth and get some air. You know it's awfully hot in New Grandma's apartment. Don't you like to go swimming when you're too hot, to do something to cool off?"

"I don't like them teeth," Josh said. "They scare me."

"Have you spoken to New Grandma about those teeth?"

"No."

"Have you spoken to the teeth themselves?"

"No."

"Maybe you should. Maybe you should ask those teeth to tell you about some of the secrets."

"Like what?"

"Like why it's always so hot in New Grandma's apartment."

"That's not really a secret," Erik said. "Everybody knows why it's hot: because New Grandma is always cold. But I don't want to know her secrets. If I did, they wouldn't be secrets."

"That's a good point. You are two very smart little boys," I said. "I'm proud of you."

"I don't want to go into that bathroom again," Josh said, "I'm scared. I don't want them teeth jumping out of the glass. They might try to bite me."

"But what if you have to go...wee-wee?"

"Then New Grandma will have to take the teeth out of the bathroom and hide them or put them back into her mouth."

"Maybe you should tell New Grandma how you feel."

***

The next day while at our daughter Heather's house, the two boys and I composed a poem:

On a visit to New Grandma's
Josh had to pee
But he couldn't
use the bathroom
because the secrets were free
The teeth was a chomping
And acting the meanie
Josh was afraid
they might
bite off his weenie

The two little boys found the poem very funny and committed it to memory. When they next saw New Grandma they recited it for her. New Grandma wasn't amused. She didn't say anything, but remained stone-faced.

Months passed. The poem was forgotten. Little boys have a short attention span, but not old ladies. They're like elephants, they never forget. One night while eating dinner, Hannah turned to me and said. "New Grandma is still angry with you for writing that poem."

"You're kidding?"

"No, I'm not. She's furious."

"It was just a silly poem—a joke. I wrote it to make the boys laugh. They thought it was funny."

"It's not funny. Not to New Grandma. She says you were insensitive and cruel."

"No I wasn't. I was just fooling around. They're children. I can't believe she even took it seriously."

"She did, and still does."

"Gosh, I'm sorry. Do you think I should

apologize?"

"That would be a start. I doubt if it would do any good, but it wouldn't hurt. On the other hand, maybe we shouldn't bring the subject up again. It might be like pouring gasoline on a fire."

"Yeah, don't poke the bear. Is that what you're saying?"

"Yes—that's it, exactly."

"I guess I miscalculated. I never would have thought New Grandma would take offense at something so ridiculous and childish. I didn't mean anything by it. I was just playing with the children. I didn't give it a second thought."

"I know, but New Grandma is sensitive. She doesn't want any attention drawn to her—not even in jest. She feels hurt."

"I will try and remember that. I won't say anything to her now about it, and I won't let anything like that happen again. I promise."

"I think that is a good idea," Hannah said. "Thank you."

Two-year-old, Josh, goes for the milk.

CHAPTER SIX

A Smoker's Legacy

One evening we were sitting at a restaurant, trying to coax Marilyn to eat. She cut her potato in half and then cut one half into two pieces. She was working on eating her ¼ potato, when she put down her fork and looked directly at me. "I don't appreciate what you did a few days ago."

"What did I do?" I asked sheepishly.

"You told the grandchildren if they smoked cigarettes they would end up like me."

"I said that?"

"Yes, and I don't appreciate it. First you write that stupid poem about my teeth, and now this."

"I'm sorry. I was only trying to make a point. I don't want them to start smoking. They are at an impressionable age and easily influenced. They might think smoking is cool."

"You didn't have to use *me* as an example."

"I guess not, but they know you. They love you and see you frequently."

"It doesn't matter."

"They see you carrying around that oxygen tank and how hard it is for you to breathe. You can't go ten steps without becoming exhausted. They've asked me why you are always out of breath. I was trying to explain the consequences of smoking. That's all. I thought it was a teachable moment."

"I am not an example: that's what I object to. And besides, I don't smoke."

"You don't smoke *now*, but you smoked for a long time, about fifty years. That's a lifetime. You have emphysema. That's why it's so difficult for you to breathe."

"No, I don't have emphysema."

"Of course you do. If you don't have emphysema, then what is wrong with you?"

"Bronchitis. I had a cold last year and I developed a touch of the bronchitis. Since then, I've had a little difficulty breathing. And what would you know about it anyway? You're not a medical doctor."

"Marilyn, your lungs are damaged. You smoked

for a long time and that's what happens. Behaviors have consequences. Look at what happened a year or so ago in Ferguson, Missouri."

"What do you mean?"

"I mean the people who burned down their community."

"The protestors?"

"Yes. The people carrying those signs that say, *Hands up...Don't shoot*. They protested, looted, and then burned their own community down."

"Wasn't that because a policeman shot down an unarmed Black man on the street?"

"Exactly. But why? It wasn't like it was hunting season on Black men. No, the victim, Michael Brown, was stopped by the cop for stealing cigars. That was the root cause. The police officer confronted him. He charged the officer, and then was shot down like a dog. The grand jury didn't issue an indictment. They felt the officer was acting within accepted police parameters. The people didn't agree. They got angry and took to the streets. They looted, and destroyed everything in their path. Remember how the stepdad of the boy kept jumping up and down screaming, 'burn the bitch down.' The mob listened and then they decided to take stepdad's advice. They burned the bitch down—the bitch being their own community. It's the domino effect; one domino falls over and knocks over another, which falls and strikes another domino and so forth. It's a chain reaction. But there is always a cause—there's always a first domino. Behaviors have consequences. In the case of Michael Brown it was stealing cigars. In your case it was smoking cigarettes. You developed a condition. It's called emphysema. You know what people say, a rose by any other name would smell just as sweet. "

"Roses don't smell. That's how much you know. Do you know why roses don't smell?"

"No idea. Tell me."

"Because in the effort to develop a strong, healthy plant, one that can be shipped thousands of miles around the world they inadvertently bred out any characteristic fragrance. Wild roses have a scent; roses that you might encounter growing by the side of the road, but domestic, long stem roses, forget it. They may be beautiful, but they don't have a fragrance."

"How do you know this?"

"Because I'm not just old, I'm smart."

"Whatever! You know what I mean."

***

The following evening, our daughter, Heather, brought her children (our grandchildren) to the house to watch a movie. Marilyn wanted to see the movie too. She came into the room with the plastic tubes inserted into her nostrils. Hannah followed behind lugging the breathing machine. It wasn't the portable unit Marilyn usually wore slung over her shoulder. It was the big box that plugged into an electrical outlet. The machine was about 2′ high, and 8″ wide. It wasn't quiet, but made a buzzing sound, like a piece of industrial equipment.

Because of the noise, it made watching a movie difficult. We had to turn the audio up and put on subtitles. After about ten minutes, one of the little boys, Josh, who was five years old, turned to New

Grandma and said, "New Grandma, can't we turn that buzz-box off? It's loud and it's hard to hear the movie."

Marilyn was speechless.

Hannah immediately sprang into action and replied. "I'm sorry Josh. New Grandma needs the box to breathe. You wouldn't want her to be uncomfortable, would you? Try to imagine how hard it would be if you couldn't breathe. It would be terrible."

"I had a fish once that couldn't breathe," Josh replied. "It jumped out of the bowl and flopped around on the floor. It was a goldfish."

"Well, you can see then how awful it was for that poor fish. I hope you put it back in the water."

"Yes, but it was already dead. I watched it bounce for a while and then it died."

"Josh, that's terrible. You wouldn't let that happen to New Grandma, would you?"

"No, because she's not a fish. But she shouldn't have smoked those cigarettes. They're not good for you. That's what Grandpa Daniel says. He calls cigarettes cancer sticks. Sometimes he calls them coffin nails. He said if New Grandma hadn't smoked, she would breathe better. Then we would be able to hear the movie."

It was too much for Marilyn. Her feelings had been hurt. Josh's remarks stung. To New Grandma, it was a rejection. She glared at me. "See what you've done. You poisoned their minds against me. Your remarks about my breathing caused Josh to say those awful things. I'm going to my room. I don't want to spoil everyone's evening."

Hannah stood up. "Don't be silly, Mom. He's just a little boy. He's five years old, and he doesn't know better. We can hear the movie just fine. Isn't that right?"

"Yes, New Grandma." Everyone spoke in unison, like a Greek chorus. Even I was supportive.

"I don't care. I want to go to my room. The children have learned Daniel's lesson. Smoking is bad. I get it. I shouldn't have smoked. But I did, and now I'm sorry. I don't want to keep everybody from enjoying their movie. I can read in my room."

"Josh," Hannah said. "Apologize to New

Grandma. You've hurt her feelings."

"I'm sorry New Grandma," Josh said. "I didn't mean to hurt your feelings."

"It's all right, Josh," New Grandma said. "My breathing machine is noisy. Maybe someday someone will invent a machine that is quiet. Until then, I will be happy to read in my room. I like reading. You go ahead and enjoy the movie."

"You know, Josh," I interrupted, trying to be a peace-maker, "It's really not New Grandma's fault that she smoked. New Grandma is old. When she started smoking, nobody knew it was bad for your health. When she was young, all the actors and actresses in the movies smoked. Practically everyone smoked and nobody said anything about it being bad for your health because nobody knew. And that's when your New Grandma started. So you see, Josh, it's really not her fault."

Josh looked at New Grandma and apologized a second time. "I'm sorry New Grandma. It's all right if your breathing machine makes noise. I'll listen better. You can stay for the movie."

"Thank you Josh, but I think I'll just go and

read in my room. I actually prefer reading." And with that, New Grandma rose to her feet, collected her plastic tubing, and shuffled out of the room. I offered to carry the breathing machine for her, but New Grandma glared at me and then hissed, "Not you, I want Hannah to do it."

CHAPTER SEVEN

The Blackened Toes Incident

Marilyn was admitted to the hospital for a surgical procedure to correct another vascular condition. While in recovery she was tethered to a machine which monitored her vital signs. A saline drip was inserted into the back of her hand and oxygen tubes dangled from her nose. Hannah sat in the room reading an old issue of *Good Housekeeping*.

Marilyn had been resting comfortably in the twilight state between sleep and consciousness. Occasionally the monitoring device would beep, or hiss, and every time it did, the old lady would sit up, reach for the television zapper and put it to her ear.

"Hello. Hello, is anybody there? I can't hear you. Please speak louder."

"Mrs. Miller," the attending nurse said, "nobody

is calling you. That's the control unit for the television. It's not a telephone."

"Yes, Mom," Hannah said, putting down her magazine. "It's not a telephone."

"But it's ringing. I can hear it." Marilyn was adamant. "My toes are blackened and someone keeps calling me." After receiving several *telephone calls*, Marilyn finally relaxed and fell back to sleep.

She must have been dreaming about having dinner in town because suddenly she sat bolt upright and began to pull the IV tubes out of her hand.

"I have to leave. I need to get out of this place," she said.

Hannah was alarmed and called for the assistance of the nurse who returned to the room and said, "Mrs. Miller, you must not do that." She tried to restrain Marilyn.

"I'm going to the *Red Lobster*," Marilyn said. "My daughter is taking me."

"Mrs. Miller, you're in the hospital and are a little loopy. It's the medication. You need to rest now. Later you can go to the restaurant." She gently pushed Marilyn on her back and began to attach the tubes again. Hannah returned to her chair.

But Marilyn was agitated. She began to thrash around, swinging her arms in all directions. "Did you call the police on me?" She screamed at the nurse. "Are they coming to get me?"

"No, Mrs. Miller. Nobody called the police. You're quite safe here. You need to rest."

Marilyn tried to sit up again, but she was so frail the nurse easily held her down. Then the nurse called for assistance and a male nurse entered the room.

"Oh, so you're the police," Marilyn proclaimed. "Are you coming to take me away?"

"No, ma'am" the man replied. "I'm a nurse, too. There are no police here. Nobody is going to take you anywhere. You're in the hospital and you're a little confused. You need sleep."

"I don't want to sleep! I just woke up, damn it. Besides, I have blackened toes. How can I sleep with a police record? Don't you know a police record can follow you throughout your life?"

"Nobody is going to have a police record. Just try to relax. Your toes will return to normal. They are only bruised. Your daughter is here with you now and she says she will stay with you."

Marilyn's eyes darted around the room until she focused on Hannah. "Hi Mom," Hannah said. Then she waved. "I'm right over here." Marilyn stopped thrashing and seemed momentarily relieved. Then she smiled.

"Are we going to the *Red Lobster* now?" she asked.

"Not now, Mom. We will go later. Listen to the nurses now and try to get some sleep. Maybe tomorrow, or the next day we can go."

"Why does everybody keep telling me to sleep? I just woke up. I want to go to the *Red Lobster* and have blackened toes."

"You mean blackened catfish?"

"No, not catfish, you know what I mean... Hannah, wrapped in bacon."

"Shrimp! I think you might mean shrimp, Mom."

"Yes. Wasn't that what I said? I want shrimp,

wrapped in bacon. It tastes so good."

"Yes, Mom, I think it's the bacon that gives it flavor. I'll tell you what; as soon as you're discharged we will go to the *Red Lobster* and you can get shrimp."

"In bacon, Hannah. I don't want shrimp unless it's wrapped in bacon. It has to have bacon."

"Yes, Mom, I promise. Shrimp in bacon."

CHAPTER EIGHT

Zombie Land

More and more strange-looking people were moving into the *Canterbury Gardens*. The state relocated them from institutions throughout Michigan. The latest transfers were a group of homeless people. Some of the new tenants liked to hang out in the lobby and watch the world go by. They sat and talked to themselves, or other residents who came and went. Some folks panhandled. Many of the older residents, like Marilyn, were frightened of these people and resentful that they had been brought here.

In an effort to learn what other options were available for Marilyn, Hannah and I decided to visit a nursing home. We looked in the telephone directory and got the address of a facility in our community. It was called *Pleasant Meadows* and it was located at the edge of town.

The woman who greeted us at the door smiled and seemed friendly. She ushered us into her office and explained the policies of the home and told us they currently had two vacancies. One room had a private bath. In the other room the resident would share a bath that was located at the end of the hall. There was an entrance fee to be admitted to the facility and then monthly fees. The amount depended on which room was selected.

After the initial meeting, the woman gave us a tour through the building. It was clean although there was a strange odor that seemed to permeate everything. In a large common area there were about a dozen elderly people sitting at a table engaged in activities. Some were knitting, and others were painting. At one table a few people were being served birthday cake. They wore party hats. A staff person was trying hard to lift their spirits by singing happy birthday. Then he blew a whistle and spun a noise maker. Despite his best effort, the participants looked disinterested.

"Talk about spitting into the wind," I whispered to Hannah.

The hostess asked if we would like to see the rooms available and we answered affirmatively. She led us down the hall and showed us the vacant rooms. They were identical except that one had a private bath. As we walked down the hallway we noticed the doors of many rooms were open. Glancing inside we saw people sitting in a chair or on their bed. Most of them had the television going, but didn't seem to be paying attention. Rather, the program appeared merely as background noise. The people sat with blank looks on their faces. Some faced the TV set, others stared out a window. A few hung their heads looking at nothing in particular. They seemed dazed or heavily sedated, and reminded me of figures in a wax museum. None of the residents looked up when we passed. There was no interest on the part of the residents. Nobody offered a greeting or acknowledged our presence in any way.

After the visit, when Hannah and I had left the building and reached our car, Hannah said. "That was a terrible experience. I could never leave a person I loved in a place like that. The facility is awful." A tear slid down her cheek.

Outside, it was sunny. The air was crisp and the birds chirped. It was spring in Michigan—a good spring. "I'm glad we visited," Hannah said, "I needed to see that. It helped clarify my thoughts. The place smelled bad—a mixture of urine and cleaning products. It reminded me of a taxidermy shop or that movie *House of Wax*. It is not for New Grandma. It would kill her. If she wants to leave the *Canterbury Gardens*, she needs to move in with us. She can't live here."

"I agree," I responded, "but I don't think *Pleasant Meadows* is representative of all rest homes. At least I hope not. There must be some nice ones somewhere. And, I don't think the people inside are typical of the elderly population—even the very old. These people seemed to have given up hope."

"*'Abandon hope all ye who enter here.'* Those words were the words written over the gateway to hell."

"What?" I asked.

"*The Divine Comedy*. The epic poem by Dante

Alighieri."

"It can't be that bad?"

"It's not good."

"But to compare it to hell?"

"Maybe at a certain age hope just runs out. Maybe hell can be right here on earth. Who knows? Perhaps the vessel is empty. The soul just runs out like a glass of water with a hole in the glass. I think New Grandma would be better off to return to Florida and move to *The Villages*. Then she could take up pickleball, and dance at night in the town squares."

"Be realistic, Hannah. New Grandma has COPD. It's hard for her to breathe. She can't dance."

"I was kidding. You know, trying to lighten the mood—levity."

***

Marilyn survived her surgery and recuperated at our house. She came reluctantly. We protested, she was too weak to go home and take care of herself. In ten days she had recovered enough to return home.

"I guess I can go back to the circus now," she said, referring to the *Canterbury Gardens*. "Last month a man brought a shopping cart into the lobby. He was one of our new residents. His cart was filled with all sorts of odds and ends, including a rather good looking shoe and an overripe cantaloupe." She smiled, "At least it's entertaining there—scary, but amusing. I can sit in the lobby and watch the circus."

"Stay here with us." I responded, pouring her a cup of coffee. "We enjoy your company. And oh, I want to show you something. It was a lucky find, a fortuitous event." I went to my room and retrieved a shoebox.

Marilyn was curious. "What's in that box?" she asked. "Is it a spring-loaded device designed to scare me out of my wits?"

"Pictures. They came from an estate sale. Pictures of babies—lots and lots of babies. I don't know who these babies are. The pictures look like they were taken a long time ago. I thought maybe

Hannah's picture was among them."

"You think you're funny." New Grandma snapped. "You're not. You're just being mean and stupid, making a joke at an old lady's expense. But that's what you do. You stir things up. You're an instigator." And then Marilyn started going through the pile of baby pictures. She smiled, and then she started to chuckle and shortly thereafter we were all laughing. It was the first time we heard Marilyn laugh in quite a while.

New Grandma remembered her husband once had a bear skin. They might have used it as a photo prop. The baby could have been Hannah.

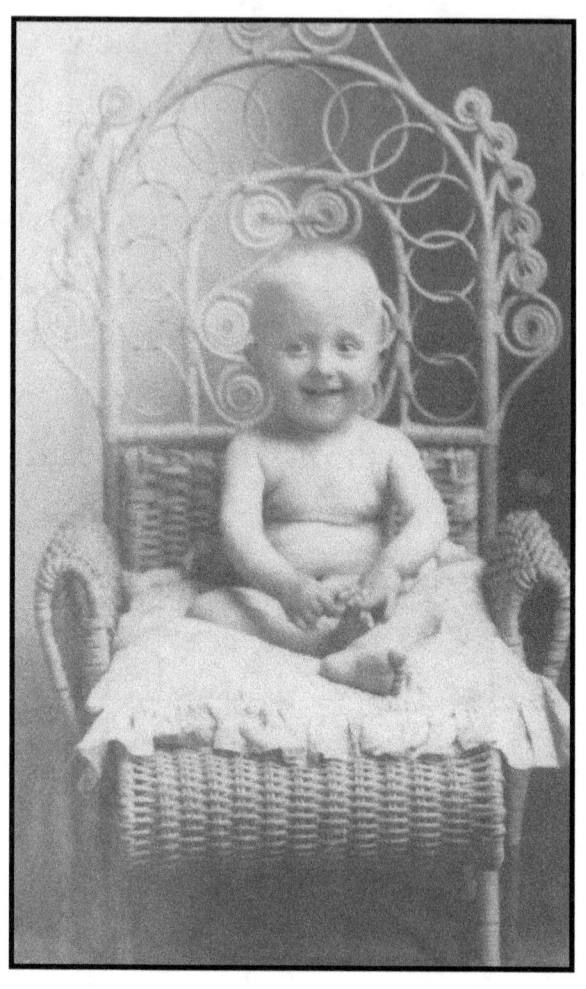

*But she also remembered having a chair
like this. And this baby looked so happy.
It probably was Hannah.*

CHAPTER NINE

More Verse

"What are you reading?" I asked.

"I'm not sure," New Grandma replied. "Maybe it's a poem. Maybe it's something else?"

"Where did you get it?"

"I found it in the bookcase, the one in the living room. It was tucked between two books."

New Grandma had been spending the weekend at our house. She was always an inquisitive woman.

"If it's a poem," she continued, "it's not a very good one. It doesn't rhyme."

"A poem doesn't have to rhyme. Besides, it probably wasn't supposed to be seen by anyone. Most likely it's just a draft."

"It's yours, isn't it?"

"Maybe."

"And, it's about me."

"No. I haven't written any poems about you."
New Grandma looked at the poem and began to
read, "*An old lady... sat on the edge of eternity...
in subsidized housing?* Give me a break, Daniel.
Are there any other old ladies around here? Who
else would you write about?"

"That doesn't mean it's about you. It could have
been inspired by you or your situation. Please, may
I see the poem?"

New Grandma handed me the paper and I
looked down at it. It was my poem. It read:

> *An old lady,*
> *neither aspiring or acquiring,*
> *sat at the edge of eternity*
> *in the lobby of subsidized housing*
> *and exclaimed to anyone*
> *who would listen, that:*
>
> *The world has turned to shit.*
>
> *It wasn't always this way.*
> *There was a time*

when the country was great.

Before the war
and the suburbs sprawled
like milk spilled on Linoleum.

Before this
internet thing
and TV violence.

I hate traffic.

Congestion subdues my patience
and children make me nervous.

I need peace and quiet.

The immigration problem
keeps me awake
at night,
but sedatives make me loopy.

You'll understand

when you're my age
and always cold.

"Okay," I confessed. "It's my poem. I wrote it."

"Of course you did. I knew that. Nevertheless, I still think a poem should rhyme, regardless of who wrote it. Have you heard of iambic pentameter?"

"Yes, I have, but I prefer free verse."

"That's because you can't write a poem the other way. To write a real poem takes discipline. You can't just blurt out whatever you're feeling at the time. That's an impression, or a rant—not a poem. Real poetry makes you think and sounds pleasant to ear."

"It's just a different style, that's all. How a person chooses to write a poem is a choice."

"Well, I'll say this about your poem, it's better than your last one, the one about my dentures in a jar. That was just plain mean, and insulting. This one, well..." She didn't finish the sentence. I interrupted her.

"I'm sorry about that, New Grandma. I was

playing with the children. I realize now that I was being insensitive. I shouldn't have made a joke at your expense. Hannah explained to me that I hurt your feelings. I never meant to. I am truly sorry."

"I accept your apology, Daniel, but I still think poetry should rhyme. Poems should be like the verse I compose for greeting cards. They should be uplifting and inspirational. They should make a person feel better."

"That is your opinion, and I agree that there is a place for inspirational poetry, but there are other forms of poetry also, written for other reasons, not just to inspire."

"Like what?"

"To make an impression, a slice of life. I see a poem like a snapshot. It is a moment frozen in time—something to return to again and again. I think of it as a way to remember what has happened, how you were feeling at the time. *Two roads diverged in a wood...and I took the one less traveled by.*"

"Robert Frost."

"Yes, it's one of my favorites, a singular moment

in time."

"*And that has made all the difference.*"

"You know the poem?"

"Of course, Daniel. I went to school. It's one of my favorite poems also. See, I contradicted myself. I get your point. It's not necessary for a poem to rhyme. I prefer it, but I don't require it. Frost's poem doesn't rhyme yet I love it. I guess I love poetry, in all its forms. I've been reading it all my life, even though I'm cold and standing on the *edge of eternity*. You know, Daniel, if you put a poem to music, you have a song. It can be a country and western tune, a folk song, whatever. Many tunes tell a story. They're all just words to music. I love words. Words have always intrigued me."

"What type of music do you like? Who are your favorite performers?"

"I used to be a big fan of folk music, especially in the 60's, during the Vietnam War era. Those were my most productive years, when I was writing greeting cards and had some measure of success. Because of the cards, I was particularly interested in words, what people had to say. I liked to listen to folk music on the radio. I liked many folk singers: The Kingston Trio, Peter Paul and Mary, but those were kind of light, mostly I enjoyed the tune. When it came to words there was a more serious group: Woody Guthrie, Joni Mitchell, Leonard Cohen, and Bob Dylan. One of my favorite was Phil Ochs."

"Who's that?" I asked. "I've never heard of him."

"He was an anti-war activist. His songs were hard-edged. He was a contemporary of Bob Dylan and Joan Baez. They were of the same generation, Woody Guthrie was older. He was an earlier generation—the grand old man of folk music."

"What was it about this style of music you liked?"

"The message. People like Bob Dylan, Joni Mitchell, Leonard Cohen—their songs said important and interesting things. Phil Ochs was angry. His songs were about social injustice, like segregation, poverty, and indifference. He was a leading activist against the Vietnam War. You didn't know me then, but I was opposed to that war. My opposition was silent, but nevertheless, I was against the war. I remember that once in the middle of the war, Phil Ochs organized a demonstration proclaiming the war was over. People ran through the streets shouting *the war is over, the war is over.* It wasn't, of course. I think what Ochs was trying to show, in a theatrical way, how absurd war was, and what a relief it would be to have it over. I mean, what were we fighting for? People were coming home in body bags—by the thousands. It was a stupid war. I think if I had been a young man at the time and had been drafted I might have burned my draft card and moved to Canada. I was grateful I only had a daughter, Hannah, and not a son to worry about being drafted."

"What ever happened to him?" I asked.

"Who?"

"Phil Ochs."

"He died."

"From what?"

"Disillusionment, mostly."

"I'm impressed," I said. "You're a complicated

woman."

"Not really. We are all like onions, with many layers." New Grandma paused to reflect. Then after a few moments she said, "Why do you want to write about me, anyway? I'm not interesting. I'm an old lady in my dotage. Does my decrepitude amuse you? Is that why you write poems about me?"

"The poem was an impression, and you're not in your dotage. You are very much alive and extremely lucid. In fact, you're as sharp as a tack. Have you stopped writing verses for greeting cards?" I was trying to change the subject.

"I haven't written one since Morris passed away. I seem to have lost the motivation. I thought of starting a journal, but even that seems tedious. I mean, what's the point? Who would read it?"

"I would. I know Hannah would. But even if nobody read it, it would still be worthwhile. It might make you feel good to write. It would be a way to remember happy times, things you might otherwise forget. It would help reduce stress. If I got you a notebook would you start a journal?"

"No. Thank you Daniel, I don't think so. I have

more important things to do."

"Like what?"

"Needlepoint. That is when I can see, which isn't very often. My cataracts are bad, and getting worse. I probably will need surgery soon. Then there's my usual state of anxiety. I worry when I watch the sideshow in the lobby. Do you remember the resident that pushes a grocery cart, the basket with one shoe in it? I think his name is Mr. Rabinowitz."

"Yes."

"Well, that man found another shoe. I don't know from where. His cantaloupe is gone. He probably ate it, but his basket now has two shoes. Of course, they don't match, and I doubt if they fit him. Why should they? He doesn't care. Why should anyone else care? What's important is that he has a pair of shoes in his cart. It's an apt metaphor for life at the *Canterbury Gardens*. Don't you think, Daniel? If you want to write a poem, write about Mr. Rabinowitz and his pair of shoes. I think that would be interesting."

Declaration Duck. A needlepoint done in 1976 by New Grandma in honor of the 200th anniversary of the signing of the Declaration of Independence..

JIM PAHZ

CHAPTER TEN

*69

One day, New Grandma had a meltdown at the Mexican restaurant. It was initiated by a remark Hannah made about the *69 technique, and how anyone could learn to use it. We had been having a pleasant family lunch when New Grandma erupted. "You don't understand, none of you. I'm an old woman and things aren't easy."

Callie (our daughter) and I were sitting across from New Grandma and Hannah. Without raising her voice, Callie objected, calmly, but firmly, "No, New Grandma, it is an easy thing to do. I do it all the time. You just have to calm down and give it a try. It has nothing to do with age. You press three numbers sequentially: the star key, then the six key, followed by the nine."

"God damn it, you don't know!" New Grandma rose to her feet. It was unusual for her to use profanity. "You're not my age. I tried that before and it doesn't work. When you are my age, maybe you'll understand."

"You mean it didn't work for you," Callie replied unemotionally. "You must have done something wrong, because, believe me, it works. I do it all the time."

New Grandma turned to me. "Daniel," she said in a pleading tone, "you understand what I mean, don't you? Maybe you can explain it to them?"

"I'm not a part of this conversation," I replied. "In fact, I was thinking of moving to another table before you start to throw food at one another."

But New Grandma wasn't paying attention to my remark. She sat back down and focused on Callie, staring her down like a rattlesnake eyes a baby rabbit. "Forget it," she hissed. "Just forget the whole damn thing." Her head started to wobble and she began to wave her arms. She looked like some kind of a weird bird of prey about to take flight. "I don't want to talk about it any more. You just don't understand. None of you do."

"Of course," Hannah said. "Let's just calm

down and let the matter drop. It's not worth getting upset over."

***

The crisis had been coming for about a week. It began when New Grandma complained that she was getting telephone calls from people she didn't want to speak with. One call was from a medical supplier asking if she needed a new meter and test strips for her diabetes.

"I don't have diabetes," New Grandma exclaimed. "I don't need supplies." She slammed down the telephone.

Then there was the representative from *TV Guide*, calling to inquire whether she would like to extend her subscription.

"My subscription doesn't run out until June," New Grandma said. The salesperson refused to take no for an answer. He told her it didn't matter that she was already subscribed; she could save a lot of money by extending her subscription.

"I'm sorry sir. I am 80 years old. I believe

the prudent thing would be to wait until my subscription runs out. Then I'll decide if I want to renew the magazine." She hung up the telephone.

The final straw, as far as New Grandma was concerned, was when the *Salvation Army* called asking for another donation. New Grandma explained she had already given, but the person on the phone asked for a second donation explaining there was a great need.

The next time New Grandma saw Hannah she complained about the telephone calls.

"These people are unrelenting. They keep calling back again and again. Can you imagine, a charity asking for more money when I have already given? What nerve! Don't they know I'm on a fixed income? What's the world coming to? But I hung up on that man selling magazines. He wouldn't take no for an answer so I showed him. I just hung up the telephone. I must say I felt a bit empowered."

"Good for you, Mom. You can stop people from calling, you know. We'll put your telephone number on the *Do Not Call list*."

A few days after her number was added to the list, New Grandma complained that she was still receiving phone calls. "Somebody from *Verizon* called and asked me about bundles. I didn't know what the man was talking about—a bundle of what? All I could think of was laundry and I know he wasn't talking about that. What do bundles have to do with using a telephone? I told him I was happy with the service I had and I didn't need a bundle of anything. Then I hung up."

"It takes a while, Mom, up to 31 days," Hannah said. "Be patient. They will stop calling, eventually. If they don't we can report them."

"How do we do that?"

"We get their telephone number."

"How?"

"By using the *69 technique."

"What's that?"

"It's a way to find out the telephone number of whoever made the last call to your residence."

But New Grandma found the concept of *69 confusing. At home she practiced without success.

She didn't mention anything more about it until three days later when she and the family were having lunch at the Mexican restaurant. That was when she had her meltdown.

The next day, Hannah asked if she had enjoyed her lunch at the Mexican eatery.

"Not at all," New Grandma answered.

"I thought the burrito was tasty."

"I did too."

"Then what was the problem? Why didn't you like your lunch?"

"It was Callie! I can't abide the way she spoke to me. I mean really! She had no respect whatsoever. I would never have spoken to an elderly person in that tone of voice. It wouldn't have been permitted. I was raised better."

"What are you talking about, Mother? Callie wasn't disrespectful to you. Callie loves you. She just said you could learn the *69 technique. It's not that difficult a thing to do."

"Well, I tried. And it doesn't work. I told you that at the restaurant. You never believe me. Nobody believes me. It might work for you and Callie, but it doesn't work for me. So it doesn't work for everybody then, does it? And I will never feel the same about Callie. She's an ungrateful child and spoiled, and you and Daniel are responsible."

"Mom, I don't agree with you. Callie didn't do anything wrong. You are just too sensitive."

"I don't want to discuss it. Let's just drop the whole matter. I know how I feel."

"Yes, Mom. Maybe that would be best. At least until you calm down."

But New Grandma didn't calm down. She apparently stewed all day and called Hannah that evening. "Look," she said, "Your daughter has no manners. She is arrogant and doesn't appreciate me. I can't believe you don't see it."

"Mom, you're being ridiculous. I think what you really mean is Callie stood her ground and didn't back down. It's OK to disagree with someone. You shouldn't take it personally."

"Of course you and Daniel will take her side. You always do. But what can I expect? You are her parents so naturally you agree with anything she says. After all, you're the ones who spoiled her."

"First of all, Mother, Callie isn't spoiled. Not by my reckoning, and she's not a child. I might add I discussed this whole episode with Daniel and he agrees with me. He felt the whole thing was silly. That's why he wouldn't participate in the argument and said he would move to another table."

"If Daniel moved to another table it would have been to take a nap. I wouldn't want to be the one to keep him from getting his rest."

"Now who's being disrespectful? Callie stood up to you and you don't like that. She had the temerity to disagree with you. She never raised her voice. She wasn't emotional, she just disagreed. And what did she say that was so bad? She said doing the *69 method was not difficult and that you could learn it. It doesn't matter that you are 80 years old now. You need to at least try and keep abreast of new technology. You're not a dinosaur, for heaven's sake, you're still alive! Look, I am going to prove you can learn this. After I hang up the telephone I am going to call your number. Then I will hang up and I want you to call *69."

"I already told you it doesn't work for me."

"I know, Mom, but just indulge me. Look at the numbers on your telephone. Do you see the button to the left of the 0, following the number nine?"

"You mean the thing that looks like an asterisk?"

"Yes, Mom, the asterisk is what is referred to as the star."

"Oh. I didn't know that. Are you sure?"

"Yes, Mom, I'm sure. What did you push before?"

"I hit 6 and then 9, and then I tried 9 followed by 6. I tried different combinations, but nothing worked. I even typed out the word STAR using the corresponding number keys."

"I see. Now listen carefully. After I make my call to you and hang up, I want you to wait a moment and then pick up the receiver. Press the star button—the one that looks like an asterisk. Then after that, press the number 6, and then press the number 9. Let's try it, OK?"

Hannah called her mother and then hung up the phone. A few minutes later the telephone rang. "It worked!" New Grandma was excited. "A nice lady came on the telephone and gave me your number. She sounded very sweet."

"It was a computer, Mom. It wasn't a real person."

"But she had such a pleasant voice. She asked me some questions like if I wanted to call you back and some other stuff. But she spoke very fast and I had trouble understanding her."

"It doesn't matter. Whatever else she said is unimportant. She gave you the number and that's what counts. That was your goal. And it worked. You got it."

"Hannah, I guess I didn't know how to do it. I mean earlier." Hannah told me that New Grandma sounded a little embarrassed. "I was wrong," she said, I owe Callie an apology."

"Mom, there's nothing to apologize to Callie for. She didn't even know you were upset with her. Now you know how to check the last number that called you using the *69 technique. You learned something new."

"The lady really did sound nice on the telephone."

"It was a computer, Mom, not a real person. It's like the lady on the GPS devise that we use in the car when we're trying to find an address. It's a voice. Not a real person."

"Oh yes, a computer. The computer-lady sounded very nice."

"Yes Mom. I'm sure whoever's voice they used was a nice woman."

***

Hannah and I thought the matter was settled. That is until some time around midnight. The telephone rang, but by the time Hannah answered, the line was dead.

"Who called?" I asked. "Who would call at this time of night and just let it ring once?"

"They hung up," Hannah said. A few minutes later Hannah answered, "It was Mother, the call came from her apartment."

"You better call her back and see what she wants. She might have a problem."

"Yes," Hannah said. She dialed her mother.

"Mom, is everything all right?"

"Of course. Why wouldn't it be?"

"Didn't you just call me?"

"No."

"Mom, are you sure you didn't call?"

"Of course not. Can't you see it's almost midnight? Why would a person call at this time of night?"

"I thought maybe you had a problem and needed assistance."

"Don't be ridiculous. What kind of a problem would I have in the middle of the night? I've been fiddling around the house, doing odds and ends and watching a little television—nothing out of the ordinary. Why do you ask?"

"Call it intuition. I'm pretty sure you did call me. You're not on *Ambien* again, are you?"

"Of course not. I'm having trouble sleeping, but I'm not taking that stuff. Don't you remember the last time I took it they found me wandering in the hallway?"

"Yes, Mom, I remember."

After hanging up I asked Hannah, "What did

your mother have to say?"

"Nothing. She denied having made the call."

"Are you sure it was her?"

"Yes."

"How do you know?"

"I dialed *69."

One of New Grandma's needlepoints.
A Renaissance motif.

CHAPTER ELEVEN

Poetry

We were having dinner one night at our house. I remember it was just a few days following New Grandma's eighty-second birthday party. My birthday present to her had been a volume of poetry entitled *A Treasury of Poems*. It was a big book and New Grandma seemed to appreciate it. On this night, Hannah had grilled hamburger patties and placed three on a platter. The buns were on a separate plate, and the table had fried potatoes, corn, sliced tomatoes, and all the usual condiments.

A few minutes into the meal and New Grandma said, "This hamburger is so good. I can't remember having such a tasty burger."

Normally, such a remark would have gone unnoticed. But on this night I looked at the table and noticed that one hamburger patty remained on the platter. I checked my own burger to confirm my senses. Then I looked at Hannah and said, "There's still a burger left. Did you cook an extra?"

Hannah opened her bun saw her burger and answered, "No, I made one for each of us."

Then I looked at New Grandma who was munching away at her burger. She seemed lost in her own world. "New Grandma," I said. "Are you eating a hamburger, or just a bun?"

She looked at me and paused, considering what I had asked. Then she opened her hamburger bun to inspect it and sure enough, no burger. She started to laugh, "Oh my goodness. No wonder it tasted so good. I thought I was eating a hamburger, but all I was eating was a bun with lettuce and tomato. It must have been the catsup that made it taste so yummy. I am a silly goose. This is what happens when you get so old you're practically a fossil; you forget even the most ordinary, everyday things." She laughed again, and then we all laughed.

"You don't have to eat the burger," Hannah said. "It's not required. You could be bold tonight, and go meatless."

"No silly. I didn't forget the patty on purpose. It was an accident. Of course I want the burger." She speared it with her fork.

After dinner, over coffee, New Grandma said, "Another ambulance came by *Canterbury Gardens* today. I think it was someone on the second floor. One of the residents told me it was a heart attack. That was the second or third visit this week."

"Visit?" I wasn't sure what New Grandma meant.

"The third time an ambulance came to take someone away. I guess that's to be expected. The average age in that place is probably somewhere in the late seventies. What does the bible say is the time allotted to man—three score and ten, I believe. If that's accurate, then most of the residents at the Gardens are on borrowed time."

"People live longer these days, New Grandma. Technology and scientific achievement have extended life spans appreciably. Besides, the bible was written a very long time ago. Things change."

"Yes, they do. And because people are living so

much longer you have an epidemic of Alzheimer's disease and other forms of dementia. Look at some of my neighbors. Longevity is not an end in itself. There must be a quality of life or existence is meaningless. I don't believe people were meant to last forever.

"Nobody lives forever, New Grandma. Death will call for all of us. We just got to have patience."

"Daniel, you know how they say when a person dies their life flashes before their eyes. Do you think that is true?"

"I don't know. Maybe."

"If it is true, I don't think people will see the big events in their life—the promotions at work, or the purchases made. I don't think they will remember the Cadillac they had twenty years ago, or the thrill they had buying it. I think what people will remember is the everyday, ordinary incidents of life. The small things, like eating a hamburger without any meat and thinking it was the best hamburger they ever tasted—silly things that don't really matter, but are stamped on our consciousness like an indelible imprint."

"Oh, I don't know," I said. "I think that hamburger was imminently forgettable. I mean in the big picture of life."

"Daniel, are you and Hannah still planning on taking that vacation you were talking about last week?"

"We are, but we haven't decided where to go yet. We wanted to do something a little different this year—something to remember. Let me show you some brochures of places we are considering." I went to the breakfront and removed the travel pamphlets. "We are thinking about the Galapagos Islands, the Amazon, and a few other places. I want to do something unique and not just go on another pleasure cruise. We've done a few of those in the past and it seemed to both of us that all we did was eat. The shows are nice, but the whole cruise experience gets repetitive and kind of boring. Besides, we've seen most of the ports of call in the Caribbean and I'm ready for something a little more adventurous. There is this thing called a Floatel, which is a hotel, built on a barge that explores the

Amazon." I started to read the brochure out loud when Hannah interrupted me.

"I remember seeing a news story about that," Hannah said. "I mean the floating hotel going down the Amazon. It was on a talk show and some actor was talking about his journey. He said it was the worst experience he ever had. The mosquitoes, he said, were as big as birds. Insects were everywhere, and he spent his whole vacation in his cabin on defense holding a fly swatter and a can of bug spray. I don't think the Amazon is the place to be on a vacation, at least not for us. I think the vacation should be exciting, but it should also be pleasant. Otherwise, I would prefer to just stay home."

"Okay," I responded. "What about the Galapagos? The ship is not a cruise ship, at least not in the traditional sense of the word. The brochures say it's an adventure cruise, and that each night after dinner a naturalist or some other scientist gives informational talks. They cover things like geography, geology, animal life, or other areas of interest pertaining to the islands. It's supposed to be an educational experience and I think it might be worth pursuing."

"That's where I would go," New Grandma said, "if I could. That sounds like a real interesting experience. If I wasn't tethered to my breathing machine, I'd go in a heartbeat."

"It does sound interesting, doesn't it?"

"Yes," Hannah agreed. "It has my vote. I'd like to see where Charles Darwin conceived of his theory of evolution."

"If you go," New Grandma said, "take a lot of pictures. I saw a television program on the Galapagos once, and the animal life is extraordinary—giant turtles, as big as my coffee table. I am a little concerned, however, about the two of you being gone. How am I going to get my oxygen tanks changed, and what if there's an emergency?"

"Callie will get you the tanks you need. She will be available if you need anything, until we return."

"Good. I won't worry. I'm sure I can rely on Callie."

"Okay then," I said. "I think the decision has been made. The Galapagos will be our destination. And we won't be more than two weeks."

"Listen, Daniel, I want to tell you again that I really enjoyed my birthday party. And I want to thank both you and Hannah for a wonderful time. The grandchildren are growing up so fast. They won't be small for much longer. Enjoy them while you can, they are wonderful. Also, I want to thank you again for the book of poetry. It was thoughtful and really is a treasure. It has all the poets I love."

"Who are your favorite poets?" I asked.

"I have several. William Wordsworth is certainly at the top of the list." Then New Grandma began to recite:

> *She lived unknown, and few could know*
> *When Lucy ceased to be;*
> *But she is in her grave, and, oh,*
> *The difference to me!*

"That's nice," I said. "Was it written by Wordsworth?"

"It was. He was prolific. I love the first verse from his *Ode on Intimations of Immortality.*

> *There was a time when meadow,*
> *grove, and stream,*
> *The earth, and every common sight*
> *To me did seem*
> *Apparelled in celestial light…*

"The poet is reflecting on his youth," New Grandma said. "I think we can all relate to that. It's a long poem, but beautiful. I love it."

"Can you recite the whole poem?"

"No, Daniel, just the beginning. But I can read it. And with the book you gave me, I can read it again and again. There are other poets I admire almost as much—poets like—Robert Frost, T.S. Elliott, The British poet Lewis Carroll, and the Irish actor Pat O'Reilly. My list is long. I have eclectic taste."

"Didn't Lewis Carroll write Alice in Wonderland?"

"Yes, but the correct title is *Alice's Adventures in Wonderland.* Carroll created the genre of nonsense poems. He is fun to read."

"And who was the other fellow, the Irishman? I don't believe I've ever heard of him."

"He is a person who wrote a poem about mothers. I dearly love his poem. It speaks to my heart, and reminds me of my own mother."

"Maybe someday you might like one of my poems," I said. "I've written lots of them."

"I know, Daniel—teeth standing at the edge of eternity. I remember; a little less than inspiring."

"What is it about poetry that you like so much?"

"It's a way to remember. When Wordsworth reflects on youth we can all relate to those feelings—they are universal. The same is true with O'Reilly's poem about mothers. At my age, most of my friends and family have passed on. It leaves an empty place in the soul. Sometimes my memory needs to be stimulated and that's what poetry does for me. It helps me to remember and to feel intensely. It makes me appreciative of being alive. I might try to write a poem about that meatless hamburger. Here's something to ponder.

If a hamburger doesn't have meat, is it really a hamburger or is it just a wanna-be sandwich?"

"That's a tough one, New Grandma, a real conundrum. I'll have to give it some thought."

*One of New Grandma's earliest and
more whimsical needlepoints
was of a rooster.*

CHAPTER TWELVE

Illness

For the next three years New Grandma chugged along like my old Buick. She had some minor complaints and her ups and downs, but she kept going. During the summers we continued to have our travel adventures although it was getting harder for New Grandma. After she was diagnosed with COPD and had to lug around the oxygen tank she appreciably slowed down. Then, one day about eight years after New Grandma came to Michigan, she stopped eating. It wasn't a deliberate decision. It was unspoken, and came from somewhere deep within her. New Grandma was now 85 years old and her weight had dropped to 86 pounds. Hannah and I were alarmed. We had been nagging her to eat since she first arrived in Michigan. But this time, something was different.

In addition to her emphysema, she had

contracted a head cold which developed into bronchitis. It left New Grandma exhausted and more breathless than usual. She spent two days in the hospital.

After she was discharged, Hannah decided to bring her mother home so she could nurse her back to health. It was demanding work and New Grandma didn't seem to want to cooperate. She refused every attempt to get her to eat. When a meal was placed in front of her she would mash it up and move it around with her fork. Then she would indicate she had eaten enough and didn't have an appetite. No matter how much Hannah or I tried to coax her—nothing worked.

"Why won't you eat?" I asked, exasperated. I was pleading.

"I'm not hungry," New Grandma responded.

"But if you don't eat you will die. That should be obvious. Two-plus-two equals four. If you don't get the nutrition your body requires it will shut down. You will starve yourself to death."

"I guess." New Grandma was listless and not interested in the conversation.

"Do you want to die?" I asked.

"Of course not," New Grandma snapped.

"Then maybe you should look at food as medication. Make yourself eat so you can get better. Think of each bite as taking a dose of medicine."

"I'm improving," New Grandma said. "I'm getting stronger every day."

I knew that was a lie. Everybody knew.

Earlier in the day, when we were alone, Callie had said, "This is what old people do before they die. I see it at hospice all the time." Callie, had been doing volunteer work at hospice. "I think it is the body's way of letting go, of telling you your time is almost up."

"It is heartbreaking," I said. "I can hardly stand to watch, and it's devastating to Mom."

"Yes, it is," Callie replied, "but it's normal. Death is only the end stage of life. It happens to us all."

***

And so began the painful process of watching

New Grandma fade away. Two days after the conversation with Callie, New Grandma could no longer walk to the bathroom. We rented a port-a-potty, a chair that was kept by her bed. When she needed to use the toilet, Hannah would put her on the chair. When New Grandma was finished Hannah would carry her back to bed.

Most nights, New Grandma stayed awake. She complained that she couldn't find a comfortable position. Hannah slept next to her. Every hour New Grandma would complain she needed to go to the bathroom and Hannah would have to put her on the port-a-potty. She would sit there for 20 minutes or so.

New Grandma was now complaining about everything, but especially about her medication. She couldn't understand why she needed to take so many pills. With each passing day, she became weaker and more distressed.

Hannah was at her wits' end. She was deprived of sleep and constantly called upon to attend to her mother. When it was obvious that New Grandma continued to decline, Hannah called for an emergency appointment with New Grandma's physician. When Dr. Goldfeder examined her, he indicated she needed to be back in the hospital immediately. X-rays revealed that New Grandma had pneumonia and she was put on different antibiotics than what she had previously been given for bronchitis. The medicine gave her diarrhea.

After a three-day hospital stay New Grandma was moved into a rehabilitation center named *Merciful Care*. By the second day she hated the place and wanted to be moved to another facility, one which was closer to the hospital.

"They are mean to me here," she said. "If I ring the buzzer it takes them ten minutes to answer. That is too long. Besides, people are walking up and down the hallway during the day and night. I want to be closer to the hospital in case of an emergency. One man keeps stopping by my room and looking in. I think he's a cowboy. Last night he came with a guitar and asked me if I wanted him to play. I told him I didn't want any music and after he left I called for the nurse and asked her to keep my door closed. The man frightened me."

"The people walk up and down the hall for therapy," Hannah said. "They don't have a rehabilitation room here and the best type of therapy is walking. People are encouraged to walk. It speeds their recovery. I'm sure the cowboy was only trying to be a nice man."

"I don't care. I hate this place—what with their cowboys and what not. I want you and Daniel to move me to that other facility, the one next to the hospital."

We arranged for New Grandma to be transferred to the facility connected to the hospital. Upon her arrival it was explained to us that she would have more extensive treatment. A team would evaluate her and a conference was scheduled in two weeks to assess her recovery.

Initially, New Grandma was happy, at the new facility, but by the second day her complaining began anew.

"These aides don't know what they are doing here. They're ignorant. I don't think they've had much schooling or special training. I believe I'd do better by myself at home."

"Mother, you can't go home—not yet. You first need to get your strength back. You can't even walk to the bathroom and back without assistance. Your breathing is labored. Look how you pant—even with oxygen."

"I'm not happy here, Hannah. They brought me the wrong color Jell-O today."

"What?"

"It was yellow. I don't eat yellow Jell-O. I only want Jell-O that is red or orange."

"Jell-O is Jell-O, Mother, for goodness sake!"

"No it's not. There are different colors."

"I'll see what I can do."

"I also don't want the lights on in my room. Light hurts my eyes. There's another person behind the curtain. I believe her name is Betty. She keeps her television on all night. I can hear it. It's not loud, but I don't want to hear anything. My ears are sensitive. Even the slightest sound bothers them. Can you get her to turn her sound off?"

"No, Mother. I have no authority over Betty. She's not telling you what to do. She has the right to watch television if she wants to, even during the nights. The speakers by your pillows are individual speakers. There is hardly any sound. Try not to listen so hard. Ignore her."

"Sometimes I hear Betty crying behind the curtain. It bothers me and I feel sorry for her."

"That's sad, but we don't know anything about her, or her situation. It's not your concern. Worry about your own recovery. Forget Betty. Try and get some rest. Let's work on getting well."

As the days passed, New Grandma became increasingly irritable. Hannah spent most of the day trying to persuade her mother to eat. Eating was always the big issue. Her weight had dropped to 85 pounds. With meals she would drink a beverage referred to as a "mighty shake," but she generally refused to eat solid food. There was also the matter of keeping New Grandma comfortable. Hannah would prop her up with pillows and adjust New Grandma's position dozens of times, but her mother was never comfortable.

One night when Hannah returned home she said to me, "It's like that story *The Princess and the Pea*. The one about the princess that was so sensitive even a tiny pea under twenty mattresses kept her awake. That's New Grandma. She feels everything—any fold in a sheet, anything out of place. I've never seen anyone so sensitive."

"She has no fat on her bones, no insulation. Any pressure, no matter how insignificant, is going to cause discomfort."

On the fifth day at the new facility, New Grandma became fixated on the consistency of her stools. "Tell me," she said to Hannah, "are they soft and round?"

"They look medium-soft. They're not really round, more of an indefinite, amorphous pile without shape."

"Yes, but does it look like diarrhea?"

"Not really. It's just ordinary shit, Mom."

Then New Grandma began a new routine. She would twist herself in anguish, grimace and roll her head from side to side. Sometimes she would flail and wave her arms and hands.

"Mother," Hannah pleaded, "Stop it. What are you doing?"

"Nothing. I'm not doing anything. I'm just

trying to get comfortable. I want to go home."

"You can't go home until you're well, until they say you you're ready. You're here for rehabilitation. Let's wait for your conference and see when your team says you can go home."

"*My team.* Do you know how stupid that sounds? I'm not on a basketball court. I would do a lot better at home. I could put a porta-potty beside the couch and sleep on the couch."

"And who is going to empty your potty, me? Who will help with cooking and cleaning and getting your medicine? You can't be home alone."

Hannah's response didn't sit well with New Grandma. Like all concerns or criticisms, she interpreted it as a personal affront. She began to shake again, going into her pre-flight mode. Then she began to pant resembling a fish out of water struggling for each breath.

"Stop it Mom! Stop panting like a dog. Breathe through your nose. The oxygen is going into your nose. It doesn't do you any good if you don't breathe. Don't gulp the air. Calm down and try and get yourself under control."

But New Grandma was by now quite beyond herself. She continued flailing, and blasting off into her own personal stratosphere. She was having a panic attack and beyond following instructions; she probably hadn't even heard Hannah's words. A nurse had to be called to administer a sedative.

CHAPTER THIRTEEN

Who's Evaluating Them?

The two weeks until New Grandma's conference passed slowly. Each time Hannah arrived, her mother would say, "Thank goodness you are finally here." Then she would show Hannah her notepad where she had scribbled an agenda as well as complaints that had arisen during the night. Hannah arrived at 7:00 am and stayed until 9:00 at night, with a 2-hour break in the afternoon.

"Well, I am here now," Hannah would say. "How are you doing today?"

"Very well. I believe I've much improved. I think I'm ready to go home now."

"We'll see. Let's wait until your evaluation and see what your team says."

"And who's evaluating them?" New Grandma snapped. "I don't really care what the so-called *team* thinks. It's what I think that's important. It's me lying here—not them. If I could just sleep in my own bed at home I would be more comfortable. I breathe better at home. They tell me now that I need to sleep sitting up, because I shouldn't put pressure on my lungs. But at home, I know I could sleep. I'm certain of that."

"Mom," Hannah responded, "it's not time yet." Hannah was exhausted. "We've had this conversation before. Every day we have this talk. Let's wait until after your conference and then we will see what's best for you."

The day of the conference did not start well. That morning Hannah went to the facility to help her mother eat breakfast. The previous night New Grandma had developed a bedsore. A wound specialist was called and ordered an air mattress to be placed on New Grandma's bed. When Hannah arrived, the air mattress had been delivered, but not yet put on the bed. New Grandma was livid.

Hannah tried to get her mother to eat some breakfast. New Grandma sat upright on her bed and pushed her food around the plate as usual. Forty minutes later, Hannah pointed out that New Grandma still hadn't eaten anything. Her mother snapped. "It's cold. This food is cold, and I don't like cold food."

"It wasn't cold when they brought it."

"Maybe, but it's cold now."

"Okay," Hannah said, defeated, "Why don't you lie down and rest."

"No, I'm not lying down. I'm not moving from this spot. I'm waiting for my air pad to be put on the bed."

"Mom, they will do it, eventually. They're probably occupied with some other things. Stop worrying about it."

"You don't know what it's like. I'm in agony. The sore on my butt hurts—especially when I put pressure on it. Anyway, you don't have to stay here,

Hannah. Go home. I know you have other priorities. I wouldn't abandon you, but I don't expect the same from you—not you. So go. Leave me with these people—these students. Oh yes, do you know that? These 'workers' are students. It seems this is a training hospital and these youngsters are getting trained. But right now, they know nothing. So that's probably why they send them here to help me. But they are no help. They are ignorant. They aren't any better than those idiots at *Merciful Care*."

A rehab worker appeared to remind New Grandma it was time for her rehabilitation. "No," she hissed. "I'm not doing rehab today. I'm waiting for my air pad to be put on the bed—maybe later." The rehab worker shrugged and left the room.

"I'm sorry, Mom. I'll see you later at your conference. I'll stop by the administration office on my way out and tell them you're still waiting for your air pad to be installed." Hannah left. She stopped at the office and gave them her message about the air pad.

When she reached the parking lot and got into her car she just sat there and cried. *Why isn't my mom improving?*

CHAPTER FOURTEEN

The Conference

Five hours later, Hannah and I entered the rehabilitation facility. We were directed to a meeting room where two men and a woman were waiting. They each introduced themselves. One was a nurse, and the two men were social workers. They explained they would review the rehab plan for New Grandma. There was a knock on the door and a rehab worker entered, pushing a person in a wheelchair. The individual looked incredibly old, was ashen-faced, and extremely emaciated.

I was the first to notice. "There's been a mistake. I don't think this is Mrs. Miller," I said. "That person is a man."

Hannah was still staring at the figure, trying to decide what was wrong with the image sitting before her in the wheelchair. The person was skeleton-like and the hair was the same length and color as her mother's, white with a tinge of gray. But when Hannah heard my words she realized immediately I was correct. "That's not my mother!" she exclaimed.

"Oh my goodness," one of the social workers said, "of course not," he stammered. "That is Mr. Teagarten." He looked down at his pile of papers and found today's schedule. "Mr. Teagarten has an appointment at 2:00 p.m. It is only 1:30 now. This is the time reserved for Mrs. Miller." He turned to the worker pushing the wheel chair. "Please take Mr. Teagarten back to his room, and bring down Mrs. Miller." The man turned to Hannah and me, "I'm so sorry. This sort of thing sometimes happens." He paused, reviewed his notes, and then continued. "Mrs. Miller refused therapy today. You should be advised that if a person refuses therapy for three days in a row, Medicare cuts them off financially. Your mother won't be allowed to stay here unless she cooperates and continues to have therapy."

"I see," Hannah said. "I'll be sure to tell her so she'll understand."

The attendant from the rehabilitation department returned with an empty wheelchair. "Mrs. Miller says she doesn't want to attend."

"That's what I'm talking about," the social worker added. "It's a spirit of non-compliance. But we can continue without your mother. Tell us, what do you see as an ultimate goal for her?"

"Are you kidding? To get well, of course. To be able to leave here and return home."

We continued to discuss what we considered optimum for New Grandma. We were talking when the rehabilitation worker returned, pushing New Grandma in a wheelchair.

"I'm sorry," New Grandma said in a whispered voice, "I misunderstood. I thought they wanted to take me to therapy. I didn't realize it was for this meeting. I know this is important and I am here now."

"That is good, Mom, because we need to talk about your rehabilitation. You need to know, if you refuse your rehab they are going to kick you out of here. Medicare cuts you off financially if you refuse."

"What will happen to me if I leave? Can I go home to my apartment?"

"No, Mom. You can't go home until you're well. You need to be able to take care of yourself. Dr. Goldfeder must write a recommendation. If you don't recover enough to go home, you will have to go to an assisted living facility—a nursing home."

"I see." New Grandma thought about what she just heard. "Okay, I understand. I will cooperate with the rehabilitation. I'll be good and behave myself."

"Thank you," Hannah said. I could hear the relief in her voice.

***

The air mattress was finally put on the bed, but of

course, it didn't work—not at first. New Grandma could not get comfortable. The nursing staff spent a lot of time tinkering with the mattress, releasing air, trying to make it softer, but New Grandma's skin was too sensitive, and she bruised easily, it was impossible to make her comfortable. The staff raised and lowered the bed, and did everything they could do to accommodate their patient. Finally, New Grandma accepted it. There wasn't much else she could do and she had no fight left in her. By now she had developed a second bed sore.

CHAPTER FIFTEEN

Atavan

During New Grandma's stay at the rehab facility, the most difficult time for her was being put to bed after a trip to the bathroom. She didn't actually climb into bed herself, but was assisted by two workers. She had two bed sores on her buttocks which caused a great deal of pain. The treatment was to position her on her side, apply a cream or bed sore patch, and to utilize the air mattress. Her pillows needed to be adjusted and the whole ordeal left her breathless and exhausted. New Grandma could only lie on her back. A rolled up blanket was rotated side-to-side to prop her weight off the sores. The measures helped, but only to a limited degree.

A good barometer to New Grandma's level of comfort was whether she kept her eyes open or closed. If she was feeling better and had an optimistic attitude, her eyes would be open. When she felt bad or discouraged she kept them closed. Sometimes she would keep them closed for hours.

"Open your eyes, Mother," Hannah would plead in frustration. "I know you're in there. I want to talk to you and I want you to acknowledge me. That can only happen if you are looking at me."

New Grandma would reluctantly open her eyes. "What?" she would ask. "What do you want?"

***

Around the third week of rehabilitation, New Grandma developed an irrational fear of falling out of bed. It was pointed out to her that the bed had rails and that she was surrounded by pillows, but the fear persisted. Hannah kept trying to reassure her that her chances of falling out of bed were about the same as being struck by a meteorite.

One afternoon Hannah told her mother she had been talking to the people from the beauty shop located within the facility. "I was trying to schedule an appointment for you to have your hair done. They do hair on Thursdays and Fridays. I made a tentative appointment for next week."

"Why can't they do it this afternoon? I want to go today."

"It doesn't work that way, Mother. It's not the same as when you are in your apartment and can call a beautician for an appointment at any time. They do hair here only on Thursdays and Fridays. We must wait until it's convenient for them, and they can work you into their schedule. There are lots of patients who want to get their hair done."

"I don't understand," New Grandma whimpered; she began to tremble. This had become her usual response whenever she became frustrated or disappointed. After she settled down, she began to compulsively rearrange the items on her bed tray—medicines, a box of tissues, a note pad for her random thoughts, and a cup of ice water.

Hannah came to realize that arranging all the items in the right position on the tray gave New Grandma a sense of control over her environment. It helped to make sense of the reality in which she now found herself. She couldn't control much in this new world, but she could control where the items were placed. Any change from the ordinary routine or what she expected caused New Grandma a great deal of anxiety. That was why the discussion about her hair appointment was so unsettling. This type of thinking was not limited to the items on her tray, but also to the arrangement of her pillows, and whether or not her sheets were straight.

For the first three weeks that New Grandma underwent her rehabilitation, she was angry with everything and everybody. According to New Grandma, the staff was incompetent, the bed was too hard and too high off the ground. Food was unpalatable and tasted like cardboard. Her treatment schedule was always unpredictable. Nothing happened the way it was supposed to happen or when it was supposed to happen. New Grandma had plenty to complain about. Hannah listened patiently, even when she was the object of her mother's dissatisfaction. Hannah arrived early each morning to help her mother eat and get ready for the day. Then Hannah returned in the late afternoon (after New Grandma's nap) and stayed from dinner until bedtime. Hannah helped with all aspects of her mother's care from dressing to cleaning dentures. At night she applied New Grandma's favorite night cream and swabbed cooling wipes on her mom's eyelids. She arranged and rearranged pillows and bed covers as instructed by her mother in search of a comfortable sleeping position, Hannah tried to remain patient and optimistic, even as her mother's complaints and crankiness increased. More than anything, Hannah wanted to remain upbeat and optimistic as she watched her mother steadily decline.

One afternoon when Hannah arrived she found her mother screaming in the bathroom. "I need help. Won't anybody help me?" New Grandma was gasping for air and swinging her arms in all directions.

"Mom! Calm down and breathe through your nose." But New Grandma kept trying to gulp air. "Stop it Mom. You're panting like a dog again. You're supposed to breathe through your nose."

"You don't know," her mother managed to say.

"I read in a magazine." Pant… pant. "Athletes breathe through their mouth."

"Mother, you're not an athlete. You have oxygen tubes in your nose because your respiratory system is compromised. If you breathe through your nose you'll get the oxygen. Then you'll feel better."

"What do you know? You don't know what it's like not to be able to breathe. You don't know anything. Call the nurse."

"Please Mom," Hannah said in an effort to calm her mother, "take one breath through your nose for me—just one. Then you can take another few through your mouth. At least do it while I'm here. Do it for me, okay? Just one."

New Grandma tried to breathe through her nose and it worked. She seemed to stabilize. "I don't know…." She stopped to pant… "Maybe," she continued, "but I read it in a magazine."

"Mom, don't you feel better now? Try another—through the nose. I have an idea. When I'm here with you, you can breathe through your nose—for me. After I leave, you can breathe through any orifice you like. If you want to pant like a dog, that's fine. You can even bark if that makes you happy. So long as I don't know about it."

"You've hurt me," New Grandma whimpered. "You hurt my feelings."

"I'm sorry, Mom, but when I see you panting it upsets me."

In order to quell her ever-increasing panic attacks, the doctor put New Grandma on *Atavan*, a mild tranquilizer. It worked well for getting her to fall asleep. The side effects unfortunately were significant. When she awoke she was addled and disoriented. Her behavior became more and more bizarre. Nevertheless, she liked the drug. Whenever she had a panic attack, she would state between gasps, "I need more *Atavan*." And the staff was willing to comply to keep New Grandma under control. The medication was New Grandma's duct tape. It literally kept her from coming apart.

One morning Hannah arrived to find her mother sitting on the bed in her underwear. "Where are your clothes, Mother?"

"Can you get my pants, Hannah?"

Hannah went to the closet and returned with a pair of pants.

"Not those," her mother snapped.

"Okay, which ones do you want?" Hannah inquired.

"Shit… Hannah, what's wrong with you? You know the ones I want."

"No Mom, I don't. I can't read your mind. Tell me which pants you want. What color are they?"

"God damn it! Why are you being this way, Hannah? I don't remember what color they are, you're supposed to know. Just forget it. Go home. Leave me. I'll do just fine right here, sitting in my underwear. Is that what you want?"

"No Mother. You know that is not what I want. I want to help you. I'll bring you all your pants and you can pick out a pair."

"A pair of what?"

"Pants, Mother. That is what we were talking about—pants."

"Can't you see how hard it is for me to breathe? What is it that you expect from me? I can't do everything. Don't you understand I have a headache? They weighed me today and I weighed 80 pounds. I've lost four pounds since I was last weighed."

"For heaven's sake, Mom. That is because you don't eat. How many times do we have to tell you to eat? We've been telling you that for eight years."

"I don't want to hear it. That's all you can say. Eat, eat, eat… like I don't already know that; like I haven't heard it a million times before. Its bullshit, and I don't want to hear it again."

**

And so it went. New Grandma became irritable, irascible, and more and more disoriented. She accused Hannah of lying, or simply not caring enough about her. Her face seemed constantly contorted in an expression of disapproval. She did everything except put her thumbs in her ears, wiggle her fingers, and stick her tongue out at her daughter. Throughout this assault, Hannah never wavered in her affection or support. She loved her mother unconditionally.

New Grandma had never been a religious person. I predicted that in her suffering, New Grandma would turn to Jesus. "You know what they say," I remarked one day, "'There are no atheists in foxholes.'"

"She's not in a foxhole," Hannah replied. "She's in hell!"

***

Sometimes, during those last days in rehab, New Grandma became frightened. She worried that Hannah might grow impatient with her, or might be too busy to come for another visit. "You will come back this evening, won't you? You promise to return? You won't leave me here by myself? I don't like being alone in this place."

"Mom, I will come back. Haven't I always come back? You don't have to worry. I will never abandon you. I promise. You're my mother."

"I know." New Grandma whimpered. Then she would tremble and start to cry. "I am so frightened," she would say, "so scared. I'm sorry I said those bad things to you earlier. I didn't mean them. It's not my fault. It's this awful illness."

"I know, Mom." Then Hannah would cradle New Grandma in her arms and hold her as if her mother was her child. "Listen to me. You're going to get better. You need to keep trying."

"I'm doing the best I can. I'm working hard."

"I know you are, Mom, and you're doing a great job. Keep it up."

One day a man from physical therapy came and demanded New Grandma lift weights. At that point she could barley even lift a spoon to feed herself.

"I can't," she gasped. "I'm too weak."

"Then you will have to leave," the man threatened. "Medicare requires you have therapy. They will kick you out."

New Grandma began to tremble. Hannah, who had been watching this exchange, rose to her feet and said, "That's enough. Get out. I will talk to her doctor this afternoon. I don't want anything else forced on her until I get back. Forget the damn therapy."

"They'll kick her out." The man protested. He had cold eyes and stood stonefaced. "I just thought she should know."

Hannah looked at him, "What part of *get out* don't you understand?"

Later, that afternoon, Hannah and I went to see New Grandma's physician. We explained that she was suffering terribly, couldn't get comfortable in bed and that the slightest pressure caused a bruise. And all the physical therapy people could think of to say was she should lift weights and needed more rehabilitation.

"Your mother is beyond rehabilitation. She is dying," the doctor said. "Her body is just giving out. She's not going to recover. I suggest you move her to hospice. They will make her comfortable and no demands will be placed on her."

"How long will she last?" I asked.

"Hard to say, it could be a matter of days, maybe a few months. Some patients actually get better in hospice, but very few."

When Hannah told her mother about the conversation with the doctor, New Grandma was thrilled. "Good," she said. "I can't wait to get out of this wretched place." Every time a nurse or rehab worker came into her room she would proudly announce, "I'm going to hospice tomorrow. I guess I won't be lifting any more weights." She said it with such joy, one would think she was about to embark on a Caribbean cruise.

New Grandma about ten years of age.

CHAPTER SIXTEEN

Hospice

Once New Grandma entered the *Woodland Hospice* she had an immediate change of attitude. Any guile or vitriol disappeared. She accepted the inevitable with a sense of calm and relief. She reminisced and talked a lot about the past.

"A man was pushing me in a wheelchair on my last day at that awful rehab place," she said, "and I passed by a picture window. I looked out and saw the sky. It was so blue. It reminded me of a trip your father and I made to Michigan after we retired and had lived in Florida for a few years. One day we both looked at the sky and your dad said, 'The Michigan sky is so blue. It is bluer than it is in Florida.' I looked at the sky and agreed. I don't know why the Florida sky isn't so clear. Maybe it is smoke from all the grass fires, or pollution, or maybe its water vapor in the air. I don't know.

But the Michigan sky is bluer and brighter, and yesterday when I looked out that window I saw it again and was reminded of that visit with your dad. I cried. But the man pushing my wheelchair was patient with me. He was a nice man and kind. I was glad to have had his help."

New Grandma smiled, and then continued, "I love this new place. The facility is wonderful and I have this whole room to myself. They let me put my favorite photos on the bedside table. Hannah fetched them from the apartment. She even brought one of my needlepoints. I made that one a few years ago. It was after our trip to Holland, Michigan. Remember? My eyes were just starting to go bad then, and the tulips were giving me a hard time. Now when I look at them it's all a blur."

"I think it's beautiful," I said. "It brings back the memory as if it was just yesterday."

"It is, Mom. It's wonderful work." Tears started running down Hannah's cheeks.

"He hung himself." New Grandma said in a voice that was practically a whisper."

"Who did?" I asked. "Who hung himself?"

"Phil Ochs."

"Really? Why?"

"I don't know, Daniel. Dissolution, I guess. He drank heavily, depression. Who knows? Maybe he was just crazy. You know, the staff is so kind and caring to me here. The medicine they give me takes the pain away, but sometimes I still cough. It's a wonderful place. I look out the window and I see grass, and trees. It reminds me of the state park Morris and I used to visit when we lived in Panama City. I believe it was *Saint Andrews State Park*. Daniel," she said, looking at me with weary eyes. "I would like to ask one thing of you and Hannah. When you go to Florida, could you visit that park in Panama City? And while you are there, could you sprinkle our ashes? We loved that place. I'm sure we would rest peacefully there."

"Certainly," I promised.

"Both of us, together."

"Of course."

"It's pleasant here. Your grandson, Kevin, came by today to visit me. And tomorrow, Hannah tells me I'm getting a visit from my sister. She is bringing her family. Hannah told me Jan might bring some of her children and grandchildren. Wouldn't that be nice? It will be lovely. You know, we are so lucky to have one another. I am so proud of our family."

That was the last thing I remember New Grandma saying. When her sister arrived the following morning New Grandma was sleeping. Jan, her husband, four of her children, and two grandchildren, all said goodbye to New Grandma. It remains unclear if New Grandma was aware of their presence. I like to think she was, but I can't be sure. New Grandma slipped out of consciousness. Early the next morning she passed away peacefully in her sleep. Hannah was by her side.

CHAPTER SEVENTEEN

Reflection

New Grandma had been an integral part of our family for eight years. Right from the beginning, our goal had been to include her in all aspects of our lives. Following the death of her husband, we asked New Grandma to come to Michigan. We tried to keep her connected to life so she wouldn't feel lonely or isolated. I believe in that respect, we succeeded. There was no family function in which New Grandma didn't participate. When we planned an event we always solicited her input. When we traveled somewhere, we always brought her with us. It was as if she had always been part of our immediate family.

Before New Grandma came to Michigan, Hannah knew her mother through childhood memories. It was a long-distance relationship with regular telephone calls. Since the time that Hannah was a child, a half of a century had passed. Hannah was now a grandmother herself, so she and New Grandma needed to get reacquainted—as one adult to another. It didn't take long for Hannah and the rest of the Savidge family to realize that New Grandma was a person like most others. She was a feisty old bird, who could be opinionated and stubborn. She loved to read, did needlepoint, and especially enjoyed shopping for office supplies. Why office supplies? Who knows? That remains an unsolved mystery. She didn't have an office or attempt to run a business.

Despite differences of opinion New Grandma might have had with Hannah or other family members over small things like cultural values, politics, or the use of technology, those differences were easily resolved. To Hannah, New Grandma was a treasure trove of information about the past and her heritage. Hannah learned about relatives she hadn't even known she had. She and New Grandma became best friends. The relationship between New Grandma and the rest of the family was also extremely positive. New Grandma became the biggest fan and supporter of the Savidge family. In her eyes, we could do no wrong, and that included me, even though she would never tell me to my face.

I suppose on some level, Norman was right when he said a mother-in-law could be a pain-in-the-ass. She could be. Even Marilyn herself admitted that much, and she did it with pride. She was her own person, and when she made up her mind about something she would not be moved.

I think about Norman's comments and the cruelty he exhibited towards his mother-in-law. I don't understand his behavior. Although I didn't fully know the relationship he had with his mother-in-law, I am quite confident Norman's attitude was wrong. I am sure to his wife, his mother-in-law was far from the detestable creature that Norman described. So what happened? Did he exclude her because she was inconvenient? Did she get on his nerves? I don't know, and never will. But it seems to me that life is like a painting with many colors. Each person we exclude from our life, for whatever reason, is a color removed from our palette. And as such, we are left diminished.

Norman's wife left him, and the subsequent divorce resulted in Norman's alienation from his only son. The boy ran off in a huff, joined the army and was sent to Iraq. One day while on patrol he stepped on an improvised explosive device. The concussive force of the bomb killed him instantly. His remains were sent home to Michigan, and a memorial service was held with words spoken of the valor and bravery of this fine young soldier. But I doubt the words were much comfort to Norman. He was a broken man, barely able to stand up by himself. He was literally held together by the support of his Rotary brothers. We were all there, the entire chapter—Norm's duct tape. *Service Above Self.*

***

Months have passed since New Grandma left us. Soon it will be years. We spend a lot of time reminiscing about New Grandma, her eccentricities, and the impact she had on our lives. "Remember…," someone will say, "how New Grandma would show her swollen foot to everyone?" And then, someone will remark, "What about the time that person appeared on TV and asked the question 'is Bigfoot in Michigan?' and little Josh answered, 'I think New Grandma is in her room.' Remember how we all went hysterical laughing?" And another person might add, "I remember how she would always say we will understand when we reach her age." And again, people chuckle and shake their heads, remembering. But deep down inside, we are just a little worried. We fear that perhaps New Grandma was right and she was privy to some secret information that we don't yet have. Maybe, when we reach New Grandma's advanced age, we will understand and the last laugh will be on us.

So now New Grandma is gone. This vital, opinionated, occasionally cranky, but oh-so-wonderful woman has left us. But she lives in our hearts and our memories, and those memories are sweet. They bring us such joy. We were blessed by her presence.

JIM PAHZ

CHAPTER EIGHTEEN

Closure

It was March on New Grandma's birthday when Hannah and I made the trip to Panama City, Florida, and the *Saint Andrews State Park*. We paid the entrance fee and parked our car. It was a pleasant day, slightly overcast, and the temperature hovered around 65 degrees. There was a light breeze, and Hannah found it necessary to wear a sweater.

We carried a cooler with drinks, and sandwiches. When we came to the picnic area, we unpacked our basket and ate quietly in meditative silence. After we finished, we walked along the beach. We came to a remote area away from any people.

"The sky is a pretty blue," I said.

"But not as blue as the one in Michigan. Remember when New Grandma told us that story?"

"I remember. Do you think we are there yet? Is

this the spot?"

"I think so." Hannah looked around. "This is a beautiful beach and a perfect day. I think we are right where we should be."

Hannah removed the two black plastic bags from her tote and gave one to me. "Before we spread these ashes," I said, "I want to read the poem by Pat O'Reilly. It was one of New Grandma's favorites, and I want to read it as a tribute to her." I reached into my pocket and took out a folded piece of paper. I unfolded it and read:

> *God made a wonderful mother,*
> *A mother who never grows old;*
> *He made her smile of the sunshine,*
> *And He molded her heart of pure gold;*
> *In her eyes He placed bright shining stars,*
> *In her cheeks, fair roses you see;*
> *God made a wonderful mother,*
> *And He gave that dear mother to me.*

We stood for a few minutes in silence. Then I said, "That was written for New Grandma." I got my pocket knife from my other pocket and cut Hannah's bag and then mine. As we slowly spilled the ashes the wind caught them and carried them, intermingling, out to sea.

"I love you Mom," Hannah said. "I love you too, Dad."

We stood together in silence. Hannah reached out and took my hand.

"So," I said, "we have kept our promise. I believe your mother was right. This is a wonderful place. She and your dad can rest here peacefully."

When there was nothing more to say or see, we turned and began walking on the beach, heading back to where our car was parked. Hannah stopped, bent down and picked up a shell. It was larger than most shells and completely undamaged. "Look how beautiful it is," she said. "I think I will take it home. It will be a keepsake, to remind me of my parents, and especially of this day. I think I will call it *The New Grandma Shell*.

"What about your Dad?"

"He won't mind. I think he would approve—it seems appropriate."

"I agree. It's a perfect shell, and perfectly named."

END

BOOKS BY JIM PAHZ
Saving Turtles
Lilith

BOOKS BY JIM AND CHERYL PAHZ
Almost Chosen...Nearly Saved
McAngel
The Last Adventure Box
Finding Quetzal
Tales of a Simple Man